# SPELLBOUND

## THE IMMORTAL LOVE SERIES
## BOOK 3

### ANNA SANTOS

Cover Design by May Freighter
Edited by Stacy Kennedy

*This is a work of fiction. Names, characters, places, brands, media,
and incidents are either the product of the author's imagination or are
used fictitiously. Any resemblance to similarly named places or to
persons living or deceased is unintentional.*

**Warning: This book contains violent and sexual
situations. Reader's discretion is advised.**

ISBN: 1540565890
ISBN-13: 978-1540565891

# CURRENTLY AVAILABLE

*Soul-Mate – Book 1*
*The Witch and the Vampire King– Book 2*
*Spellbound – Book 3*

## Coming Soon:

*Shattered – Book 4 (2017)*

---

For an updated list of books, and to have access to my upcoming releases, check my **website**:

www.annasantosauthor.com

**Or Facebook:**

https://www.facebook.com/AnnaSantosAuthor

You can also sign up for **my Newsletter** to get a notification the day a new book comes out and find more about my other books and giveaways. Join **The Immortal Love Series Newsletter**. The direct links can also be found on my website.

# BOOK DESCRIPTION

## SPELLBOUND
## Book 3 of The Immortal Love Series

Jessica is on the run, but this time she's evading her own mate so that she can secure their happily ever after.

Ruthless and biased vampire, Alaric, put a bounty on Jessica's head. She's the only one who can break his curse—or so he thinks.

The witch isn't going to wait for him to make his move. She decides to take matters into her own hands and cooks up a plan to find his whereabouts and end his reign of terror. With the help of her friends, they embark on a dangerous mission to find and kill their ruthless enemy.

Yet, despite the team's good intentions, their plan can go seriously wrong and lives might be lost in the process.

# CHAPTER ONE—AND THE QUEST FOR THE TRUTH BEGINS

Being part of a secret organization that chased and killed supernatural beings, who had the nasty habit of killing innocents for fun, gave me access to a lot of cool toys and secret safe houses. And the good thing about the safe houses was that they had places to keep special prisoners. I had a nice silver cell with matching silver cuffs for my guest. They would prevent her from using her hands, and the silver chains would keep her securely tied down, so I could begin the interrogation.

I had left Giovanna in the lounge area to wake Valentina from her defenseless, unconscious state. I didn't want her to watch what I was going to do. After all, the demoniac being was still Giovanna's mother, even if the girl seemed to be her complete opposite. It was odd that she could be Valentina's daughter. Besides, I didn't want her mom to find out the girl was helping me.

*Who knew what sordid things she could do to her after finding out?*

There were just two metal chairs and a table inside the interrogation cell. It looked like an average room in any normal Police Station. It even had an observation mirror that others used to watch the interrogation. It also had a camera, which I had turned on because I wanted proof Valentina was a liar with a hidden agenda. I could be impulsive, but I was not stupid.

And there I sat, staring at the unconscious Valentina. Even strapped to a chair with silver handcuffs and her makeup all smeared, she looked gorgeous. It was a guise to make men believe her lies. Being beautiful, I mean. They were suckers for a pretty face.

All I needed to do was wear her out until she was vulnerable to my psychic powers. Also, smack her around a bit for being a damn slut and trying to kill me. Besides, she had the nerve to try to seduce my mate. That was a really bad move on her part. If she wanted to enrage me, she had succeeded. Now, she was going to regret it.

I cleared my throat while tapping my nails against the iron table, making an annoying noise. No luck. I was going to have to use extreme measures to wake her up. I smiled wickedly. I was going to enjoy that, *a lot*!

"Wake the fuck up," I yelled, flicking my wrist. My kinetic powers threw a bucket of iced water in her face.

Valentina coughed and moaned. Her eyelids fluttered before she opened her eyes. Then, she seemed to realize where she was and who was in front of her because she tried to move her hands. Looking around, she became aware that she was handcuffed, strapped, and caged inside a room with me.

I flashed her a wide smile that made her become even paler.

"Jessica? What's going on? What do you think you are doing?" she asked, her voice laced with panic. "Turn me loose this instant!"

"Yeah, that isn't going to happen. At least, not until you give me the answers I want." I leaned back in the chair and placed my hands on my thighs.

I gazed at her, seemingly with patience, but really I was trying not to lose control and let my hands burn her, causing excruciating pain. The same pain I was feeling because I had to leave my mate and get answers on my own.

Being away from Marcus was unbearable. I had to cast a spell to prevent him from invading my mind and to stop me from wanting to go back to the safety of his arms. No way in hell was I going to let our bond allow him to find me and take me back home. I wanted, no, I needed answers and time alone to think about everything that happened between us. He had to love me for who I was and not for who I had been. But I was no longer mad at him, I was just sad and feeling lonely.

"Come on, Jessica. Do you really think you're scaring me? You can't hurt me. I was a witch like you. Your powers don't affect me. Your fire won't kill me. Don't you know that?"

"Of course I do." No hint of rage in my voice, just a fake grin on my lips. I flipped my hair and leaned forward as I laced my fingers together. "I know all about that. Because, you see, I'm not a kid anymore. I know the full extent of my powers. And I know"−I got up and walked to her− "that they may not burn you down to ashes, but they sure will hurt like hell."

Sneering, I put my opened hand on her forehead and sending my flames through her body, blazing all the way down to her feet, causing her skin to turn bright red. Valentina screamed in pain, eyes wide open in shock. She thought I was bluffing, that would teach her a lesson. I was no longer a frightened child.

I stopped the torture and brushed my hands against my coat. I cleared my throat before speaking again. "Now that we both know I'm not kidding. I would like to ask you a few questions."

I let her catch her breath because burning her meant I was burning the oxygen and preventing her from breathing. Vampires did breathe despite the myth to the contrary. I couldn't burn her to ashes, but I could kill her temporarily for lack of oxygen. And I could also badly bruise her before the healing kicked in.

She took a while to regain her ability to breathe and speak. Her blistered skin healed as she filled her lungs with fresh air.

"Damn you, Isobel. I should have killed you when I found you!" she cursed, jerking with pain in the chair and trying to loosen her hands to attack me.

I stepped back. "Then why didn't you?"

"We were friends!"

I sneered before I sarcastically asked, "That is why you tried to kill me yesterday? Because you are my friend?"

"I didn't try to kill you," she answered as if she were the most innocent person on the face of the earth and had no idea why I was accusing her.

"Of course you did! Don't play dumb with me. I'm not vulnerable to your charms, and I can see past your façade of appearing to be a helpless woman. You were the one who encouraged the rest of them to talk about my past life. You knew that Marcus and I were connected, that we were sharing our thoughts. You also knew what the amount of new memories would do to me. It would cause me to have seizures, and I could die."

"I was not trying to kill you!" she denied promptly.

"Yes, you were!"

"I was not! I confess that I did do it on purpose, though."

I glared at her with furrowed eyebrows but, at the same time, was pleased that she was admitting to it.

"But I had no intentions of killing you. I just wanted your real self to surface. I wanted Isobel to come back, so I could talk to her. She would be–easier to talk to. We are friends. I love Isobel. She would understand my plan to catch Alaric. You, on the other hand, are ruled by petty emotions."

"What petty emotions?" I asked, outraged by her words. "And what do you mean with calling my real self? I'm the real one in this body. Not Isobel."

She smiled at me with cold eyes that sent shivers of fear through my body. "Don't be silly, witch. You are just Isobel's alter ego. You aren't the real owner of that body. You're the personality that emerged after all the walls and enchantments I made to keep Isobel's memories in check. You are nothing, Jessica, and once Marcus turns you into a vampire, you will disappear for good, and Isobel will take her rightful place in that body."

I stepped back until I sat in the chair before I lost the strength in my legs. It was getting harder to breathe.

"You are lying," I whispered, barely capable of forming the words that came out of my mouth.

"You know I'm not. If you think about it, what do you really remember from when you were a kid?

Practically nothing because it was Isobel with her memories that grew up in that body."

"I remember my dad and my mom. I remember living in Australia, having friends and going to school, and the other kids mocking me and calling me vampire lover. I remember learning spells with my mom and going to the woods to learn the names of the animals and the plants with my dad. I existed before you took me away."

"Those memories belong to Isobel. You remember them because I told you to. I made you, Jessie. In the end, you are nothing but a silly girl who ran away because she wanted to see the world outside the walls of the convent. You are nothing but a slut who sold her body in exchange for vampire blood," she claimed.

I got up from my chair, stormed over to her, and slapped her across the face. "I ran away because you were keeping me away from my mate. You fucking whore!" I slapped her again. "Don't try to trick me! You locked me up in that bedroom and filled me full of pills, so I would obey you. Do you really think I bought what you said to Marcus? You had no intentions of giving me back to him."

"Of course, I didn't," she declared, licking a drop of blood from the corner of her mouth while smiling wickedly. "If I had my way, he would never see you again. And you would never see him."

I slapped her again, knowing that it was probably hurting me more than her because she was a damn vampire. I needed to change tactics before my hand got sore.

"Just tell me why." I sighed, stepping back. I pulled my chair and sat closer to her. Face to face.

Tilting her head, she asked, "Do you really want to know why?"

"No, I just kidnapped you, restrained you, and I'm asking you all these questions because I'm bored," I replied to her with sarcasm.

"You really surprised me there. I didn't think you had it on you."

"You have no idea what I'm capable of doing."

"You're right. I guess I don't. You are tougher than Isobel. She was a whining spoiled queen, always expecting someone else to do her dirty work. She had no idea how lucky she was for having a mate who loved her and protected her from everything and everyone."

"You are wrong. She knew it."

"No, she didn't. She treated Marcus like crap. She used their bond to make him do whatever she wanted. And no one could see past her manipulative ways. Even her brother loved her better than me. And I was his freaking mate!" She jerked as she tried to free herself.

I arched an eyebrow, surprised by all the hate she had cooped up inside her soul. "So you were jealous of her?"

"Not jealous. I was mad at her."

"For what?" I asked, incapable of understanding her reasons. "You found your mate, he wanted you. You have been together for centuries, why hold a grudge?"

"I was sent away from my mate because Isobel wanted me!" she yelled.

I didn't understand her anger, but I recognized hurt and pain on her features.

"I had found my mate. Francesco and I were happy. We were happy before she arrived and ruined everything!"

"What did she do?" I asked, gasping for air, afraid that I had been the one to cause discord between the lovers.

"It was a forbidden love. I knew it was. I would be decapitated if they found out I was Francesco's mate, the next king in line. I was not the right race for him. His parents wouldn't allow it, the council would sentence me to death. But he loved me. I know he did. He never told a soul about me when he found out I was his. I was fifteen. I had come to pledge an oath to the king. And then I saw him…the prince, next to his father. He was handsome, cold, and I had been taught to fear him and all his kind. And to never look a vampire in the eyes."

"But you looked him in the eyes," I guessed, caught up in her story.

"I did. His cold face and lifeless stare changed. His eyes beamed with gold, and my entire body shivered under his gaze. It was love at first sight, and I had no idea that I was his mate. But he knew. He told me a week later, after stalking me like a shadow and making me–"

"Did he force himself on you?"

"No. Francesco didn't hurt me. At least, not physically. Although, it was common for vampires to sleep with their servants. They would take witches as their lovers. And my mother always told me that my beauty would be my greatest weapon or my downfall. Besides, I was taught to obey my masters' orders. She had told me not to fight back if they tried to make use of me. I should obey their whims. I was the property of the royal family, so I had to understand that not only would they request my powers to help them with their enemies, but they would also want me in their beds. My mom was the king's mistress. It was expected that the king would…want me in his bed, too."

"That is disgusting."

Shrugging, she declared, "That was the order of things. The hard truths of the time. I had been raised to accept it. Being chosen to share the king's bed was an honor. I was just relieved when it was not the king that wanted me to share his bed, but the prince. I didn't need to pretend with him. He pleased me a lot. He was kind and gentle with me. Being his mistress meant that no one else would touch me, no one else would force their way into my bed. I was happy, I loved him. I loved him so much that I would die for him. And I thought that he loved me, too."

"So what went wrong?" I asked, emotional by the sadness in her words. She was remembering happy days, but the amount of grief that tainted her voice was impossible to ignore.

"Isobel, what else?" she asked, staring at me with murderous eyes that shifted from brown to dark.

"What did she do?"

"She came to visit us. She brought Eric to meet his family. He was a little baby. I fell in love with him. He was so cute and adorable. I was so in love at the time, I couldn't wait to be a mother. I wanted to give Francesco kids. I wanted to have a happy family just like his sister had. It didn't cross my mind that our love was forbidden, that we were never going to be accepted. If people found out I was Francesco's mate, I would be killed."

"Did Isobel find out and tell her father?" It would have been cruel if that happened, but also explained all the hate she had for my former self.

"No. She became interested in me since she was looking for a nanny for her son. She asked her father to give me to her," she said coldly, staring me in the eyes as if I was the most despicable creature in the world. And I was feeling like I was since, apparently, I was the one who caused Valentina to be separated from Francesco.

I reclined in my seat. "Isobel didn't know that you were her brother's mate, did she?"

"No. But with her pleading eyes, and being the king's favorite, she managed to convince her father to send me away to her kingdom, away from my mate."

"Why didn't Francesco prevent that from happening?"

"Because he was a liar, a prick, and he was glad to get rid of me. You have no idea how much I begged him not to let me go. I wanted to stay with him, but he said he couldn't go against his father's orders. He didn't even try to ask his sister to give up her idea of taking me away. He just stood there, doing nothing. After all the love and the promises, we had made to each other, he simply sent me away, where I couldn't ruin his plans of being the next king."

"At least, you weren't killed," I mumbled, absorbing all the information.

It was without a doubt a sad story. She had some reasons to be bitter, but everything had happened a very long time ago. She was back with her mate. Though, her story explained why she treated him so coldly. She hadn't forgiven him. He was paying for his sins. And that was why they were miserable together. It also explained Giovanna's strong animosity toward her mother.

"It felt worse than being killed," she responded with tears in her eyes—real tears that made me feel sorry for her.

"That isn't a valid reason for you to keep acting like a bitch. You have to move on and forgive your mate. And Isobel didn't treat you badly, did she?"

"No, she didn't. She welcomed me into the family as if I were her daughter. Everybody accepted me. And I loved Eric. He was my baby boy. I loved him as if I were his own mother. Despite the broken heart and the rejection, I managed to find a shred of happiness to hold on to."

"So, why the grudge towards me?"

"I've already told you that I don't hate Isobel. We were friends."

"I'm sorry, but that is not entirely true. You were trying to convince me to go to my former son's lair to kill an innocent girl and end his life. What the hell did he do to you?"

Valentina pursed her lips until she decided to share. "I was happy. I was. But I was also broken, feeling used and wanting revenge. I wanted to get back at Francesco. I wanted him to suffer as much as I had suffered. I wanted him to pay for all the lies he told me. I was a witch, so I studied every spell I could find, and there were a lot of spells in Isobel's library. I wanted to find one I could use to make Francesco pay. There was nothing in white magic, so I turned to black magic. I studied, I created new spells and magical potions. Soon enough, I was dealing with black forces that took away all my innocence and moral standards."

"Again, what has my son to do with that?"

"Alaric was away, fighting in some useless war. Did you know that he was Isobel's favorite son?"

I shook my head.

"He was. She loved him and always defended his reckless actions. He was against his family's established rules on feeding. He often disapproved of his father's decisions. But he loved his dear mother. And, by the time I was finished with him, he loved me. He is a handsome man. Have you seen him?" she asked, wicked smile drawn on her lips. I shook my head and then I nodded because I had seen him. Anna had a tape of him, killing her parents. I guessed he was handsome if one liked twisted, sick, vampire killers. "He is extremely good-looking. The only one who was not blonde like the rest. He had green eyes like Francesco. And, when he tried to seduce me into his bed, I couldn't help but see the irony in that. I was no longer a helpless and naïve young girl. I had grown up, and I knew I could control him and make him my lover, puppet, and weapon."

"So, you were the one that made my son a psycho," I declared, sitting upright and getting mad with her cruel words. *She was confessing.*

"Oh no. That was not me. That was all the blood he drank. The last thing I wanted was for him to turn out to be a vicious and crazy murderer. I just wanted him to be my new mate. Because you see, I also fell in love with him. I found out that we were alike. We had the same grand ideas and plans for changing the world. And he pleased me in bed, satisfied all of my curiosities, and all my erotic fantasies. He was also willing to get me the human sacrifices I needed to perform my black magic. Together, we could conquer the world and end the council's sovereignty. Put a stop to the killing. End the dominance of vampires over the other races. Witches are more powerful, they shouldn't be enslaved by vampires."

"You had a crazy plan to rule the world. How cliché of you," I declared with sarcasm, crossing my arms and staring coldly into her eyes. All empathy I had felt for her was long gone.

She shook her head and raised her chin. "Not to rule the world. Just balance the powers among races."

"Well, you have to explain to me how Alaric went from being your puppet and wanting to end the vampire's domination to being a crazy pureblood radical? What did you do, mix up the potions?" I asked, arching an eyebrow and smirking.

Valentina growled. Tough audience, because I thought I was funny.

"He was a fucking liar as all men in my life were. He just used me to get the spells he needed to make himself stronger. He never intended to be my mate. He just wanted to be the next king, kill his dad in the process, rule an army so he could defeat the other kings, and be proclaimed Emperor of the vampires."

"What books were you two reading?" I asked, sighing with disgust. I didn't know who was crazier, her or my ungrateful son.

"Don't patronize me. My intentions were noble, his weren't. He never intended to be my mate. He just wanted my spell so he could break your bond with Marcus."

"My bond?" I asked, blinking at her words. "Why my bond?"

"Because you were the only person he loved. He loved you, and he didn't want you to die after he killed his dad. He wanted the bond to be broken so that didn't happen. Without a bond with Marcus, you wouldn't age and you wouldn't die. I also think that he had a weird obsession with you, more than the son kind of thing, but I'm not here to judge, and I sure don't want to suggest that he suffered from an Oedipus complex." She shrugged. "But he loves you, and I really doubt that he would kill you if he knew that you were Isobel. So, I was hoping that Isobel would come back to her body, and he could be convinced that she was who she was claiming to be. Yet, you are still there, playing childish games and preventing my plan from working."

"What plan?"

"To make me his mate. *What else?*"

"Why? Didn't you just say that he didn't love you?"

"He will be forced to love me when I'm his mate."

"Oh god," I whispered, wringing my hands and rolling my eyes with impatience. "You really need to see a doctor, a psychiatrist. A really good one because you are out of your mind! You have a mate. He *loves* you! He is with you. Alaric is a twisted sick bastard. He wants to kill us all. He couldn't care less about you. And still, you want to be his mate. What the hell have you been smoking?"

The vampire glared with dark eyes. "You couldn't possibly understand. Your mate isn't a bastard. And I can fix Alaric. I have the spell to fix him. He just needs to be cured of all the blood he drank. He needs to be purged from other people's feelings, memories, and rage."

"Does your mate know what you are planning?"

"He has no clue. He thinks I have forgotten the past. But I've been waiting to get back at him. To get rid of him and of these unwanted feelings."

I sighed. My head was killing me and knowing all the sick and twisted ideas Valentina had was making me feel even sicker. They needed to have some serious intervention! In a Jerry Springer kind of way. It would be an Emmy Award winning show! I would almost laugh if it wasn't such a damn serious matter I had to deal with.

"Is your head hurting?" she asked in a honey laced voice with a smile tucked in the corner of her mouth.

"Yes, but don't be too happy about it. I'm not going to have a new seizure. I had my daily dose of vampire blood. I just think you are freaking mad, and I really need to get away from you for a while."

I got up and walked away.

"You can't keep me here forever. My mate will come for me!" she yelled before I could close the door behind me. "And he will kill you. I'll make sure of it. I'll tell him everything you did to me! You will start a damn war!

And I'll be extremely happy when all your family is killed and I take you to Alaric."

"Shut the hell up, bitch," I growled at her, sending a wave of wind in her direction.

It hit her hard, smashing her chair against the wall and shaking the building. So, I overdid it with the force I used. It was not intentional, but she shouldn't threaten my family. At least, it shut her up because she passed out. I had probably broken her neck, and it would take a while until she healed and woke up from her temporary death. Meanwhile, I needed to think about what I was going to do with her and the information I had just found out.

## CHAPTER TWO—LOOKING FOR JESSIE

### ERIC

Eric entered the palace only to be startled by his father's voice. "Where were you? Don't you know your mother is missing? What could be so important, you had to leave the palace and disappear?"

The king's voice was steady, but Eric could sense his annoyance and impatience.

"What are you doing there, seated on the chair in the hallway?"

"Thinking and waiting for you. So, don't deflect my questions."

"If you really need to know, I went to see Caroline," Eric replied, walking to his father's side and noticing his tired eyes. He hadn't changed clothes or slept by the looks of it. "When did you get home?"

"A couple of hours ago, but I need to get out of here and do something useful." Marcus got up, looking at his son who was just a few inches taller than him. He furrowed his eyebrows and placed his hands behind his back. "And this is not the time for you to visit your mistress."

"She's not my mistress. We have a no…"

Waving his hand in dismissal, he said, "Yes, a no strings attached sort of relationship. I'm familiar with the term. Still, your mom is missing and took hostages.

Couldn't that wait?"

"It could," Eric said, without breaking eye contact. "That is why I went there for an entirely different reason. Caroline is a powerful witch. She's also our ally. I took her a piece of clothing from Jessica to see if she could perform a tracking spell."

Marcus arched his eyebrow. "And?"

The feeble glow of hope was soon shattered by Eric's reply. "Jessica is too powerful. Caroline said that Jessica must have cast a strong protection spell. She can't track her. Though, she said she was going to ask for help from some of her sisters. Together, they may succeed, but Caroline looked drained when I left. I believe we won't be able to track Jessie by resorting to magic."

"Well," Marcus said, pinching the bridge of his nose, "that was useless."

"What have you been doing and where are the others?"

"I've been here trying to reach her with our mind-link. But she has blocked me, and I have no way of finding out where she is or sensing if she's okay or not." The king sighed deeply and closed his eyes momentarily. "I'll keep trying, though."

"Shane and Anna?"

"Shane is using his contacts with the police to see if he can track the car they took. Anna is with him, and she's also calling all of her contacts to see if Jessica asked them for help."

"It's our fault," Eric whispered, running a hand through his blond hair. "We nearly killed her with the memories. I can't understand how we fell for that so easily and were so reckless!" Eric circled his father and sat down in one of the chairs.

Marcus turned around to face his son. "It's not your fault. It's mine. You were a child, Eric. You barely remember Isobel. It was my memories of her, echoing inside Jessica's mind that caused the stroke."

"But why did she run away?" Eric fisted his hands. "Is she that mad at us?"

"Now that we know she left the clinic on her own accord, I must say I'm baffled by the events. But we need to consider that Jessica may have lost her memories again. She may want to take revenge on Valentina for what she has done to her in the past. Jessica may be confused, or she may be mad at us. There are too many possibilities that make my head spin. I won't give up until we find her and understand what is going on. Then, we will bring her back home where she will be safe."

"I hope so because if she lost her memories, she might not know that Alaric put a prize on her head. She might not know where home is."

"Well, she will probably contact Anna or her prior team members. Kevin has left for Chicago to talk to his former boss. He's planning to ask for the locations of the secret hideouts from New Haven to Boston and to New York."

"Why those locations?"

"We must assume she remembers the clinic as the place where Kevin had been hospitalized. Their previous headquarters were in Boston. She knows it well. Plus,

New York is a big city, and it's easy to blend in and disappear."

"I think the big questions here are, why Giovanna helped her and how long can we keep fooling King Francesco that the three of them were kidnapped? He will eventually find out that it was Jessica who kidnapped his wife."

"Francesco has his girls searching the main roads to the main cities. The GPS tracker on Giovanna has been disabled. He knows less than we do, and I made sure that the footage of Jessica's actions was erased from the clinic's database."

"Do you think Jessica will hurt Valentina?"

"Well, if she does, that vixen deserves it." The king pursed his lips and clenched his jaw. Purple flickered inside his eyes. "I'm sure Valentina did it on purpose. She knew what would happen to Jessie if there was an overload of memories. I was a fool!"

Eric got up and placed a hand on his father's shoulder. "Jessica will come to her senses and come back to us...if she remembers. And if she doesn't, we will find her and bring her back."

"She left her ring on the nightstand. If she remembers what happened, and she's mad at me because of it, she might not want to come back."

"Remembering or not, Dad, we should increase security because if Jessica does something to Valentina, Francesco will start a war."

"I should have started a war for what Valentina did to Jessica!" The king paced around with his hands closed into a fist. "I was a fool. I should have sent them away and kept Jessica safe. Valentina is hiding something, and I'm sure Jessica will do something foolish to resolve a problem she didn't create."

"Like what?"

"Like try to find your brother. She may believe she can break his curse and get close enough to kill him."

"Alone?" Eric asked, his eyes opening wide in panic.

"I'm sure she'll ask for Anna's help."

"And is Anna going to call us if she does?"

The king paused and looked at his son. "I believe Anna is more loyal to Jessica than she is to us. They are both strong-willed and hard-headed. The two of them are seeking revenge on the same killer. They want to prove to us that they don't need us."

"But they do!" Eric said, worried. "Alaric has men guarding him, probably a small army. They need us and a lot more men if they are planning to take down Alaric."

"Well, Jessica is smart, but I'm not sure if she'll be able to find Alaric's hideout. We have been looking for ages. They have been tracking his men and haven't found him. Why would it be different this time?"

"She took Valentina…"

His father frowned. "Unless Valentina knows where Alaric is hiding…"

"Alaric wants Valentina more than he wants Jessica. If what you told me is correct, it was her who cursed him in the first place."

The king nodded. "And Giovanna helped Jessica against all odds. There's something going on. I can only hope that when the time comes, Anna will tell Kevin, and he will tell us. Kevin trusts us, and he knows we are here to help."

"You should sleep then."

The king tensed his jaw before questioning impatiently, "Do you think I can sleep?"

Shrugging, Eric rubbed his temple. "I guess not."

His father narrowed his eyes. "Did the tracking spell take all night?"

"She tried other spells and incantations."

"The only incantation that woman wants to use is one for you to share her bed on a daily basis, or should I say, nightly. Have you ever entertained the idea of taking a permanent lover? It has been a while since you've been waiting for your soul-mate to show up. Maybe you should consider the idea of finding company."

"Why are you saying this?" Eric asked, frowning.

"Being lonely...can be torture."

"I'm not in love with Caroline. She's an interesting woman, but I'm not going to lead her on when we both know we are destined to someone else." Eric's voice came out more angered than he intended.

He shifted his eyes from his father who put his hand on Eric's shoulder. "I just don't want the years to come making you more bitter and lonelier than you already are."

"I'm… We are not lonely anymore. We have Anna, Kevin, and Jessie. They are family, and I'll wait as long as I need to until destiny decides to bring my soul-mate to me."

"You should get out more then." His father smirked. "She won't fall in your lap or knock on your door."

"I get out. I travel abroad, I go to reunions." Eric sighed before continuing, "You are the one who hasn't gone out in a while. I've been managing all of our family businesses."

Eric frowned at his dad who arched an eyebrow. "What?"

"You can't mistrust destiny, Dad. You used to spend your time inside your library, drawing, and dreaming about Mom. Jessie had to fall into your arms for you to see her, and in your library, might I add."

Marcus smiled. "Your mom always knew how to make an entrance."

"We will find her and talk some sense into her."

"Maybe she lost her memories of us, of me. Maybe she doesn't know we are looking for her."

Eric nodded, trying to comfort him because he knew it was too painful for his dad to think that Jessica had run away because she was angry.

"Where are you going?" Eric asked when his father stomped his way toward the door.

"Dulce caught one of the vampires who was sent here to track and kidnap Jessica. I'm going to speak to the girl and see if Jessica has contacted Sebastien. Sebastien and Jessie are good friends. We could use their help, too."

"I'm coming with you. I don't like feeling useless by staying here."

"We need to have our best men ready to leave once we know where to look for Jessica. Alaric's men may be already tracking her."

"Or she might be the one tracking and going after him. If so, she'll be putting herself in danger, and she'll need saving."

"That too!" Marcus agreed, opening the door and letting the bright light of the day in.

"I have to tell you, Dad. There's never a dull moment in this house since Mom came back to us."

Marcus smirked while going outside and calling his men to arrange a car to leave.

# CHAPTER THREE—TRACKING DOWN MYRA

## JESSICA

Jessica came out of the room with her head pounding badly and her mind numb by everything Valentina told her. She glanced around for Giovanna and found her seated on the couch, staring at a muted TV.

"Did you witness your mom's confession?" Jessica asked her.

Giovanna turned her body to watch her. Her eyes seemed vacant. "Part of it, yes. I couldn't listen to anything else past a certain point. I knew she was crazy, but I didn't know she was that mad. Still, Dad will be extremely heartbroken with Mom's intentions of getting revenge and how badly she wants to hurt him."

"She really needs help. It isn't normal to be obsessed with revenge against her mate for more than two hundred years."

Jessica sighed, feeling a shiver run down her spine by thinking about Marcus. She missed him terribly and was trying hard to keep him out of her thoughts. Yet, sometimes, in the deep recess of her mind, she could hear his voice, calling for her, begging for her to tell him that she was okay and she was going to come back home.

*Well, that was not going to happen.* He was not going to convince her to go back because she had a lot of things that still needed to be done first. Besides, he was the one failing to see the evil snake that wanted to betray them with her twisted and rather poorly conceived plan.

Knitting her eyebrows together in deep concentration, Giovanna questioned, "What's wrong?"

Jessica shrugged. "Nothing."

"Is there any more to your plan or was this it? The recording was clever and all, but it doesn't help me much. My dad will just forgive her and let it slide as usual."

Taking a seat next to the girl, she said, "I have a crazy plan. This was just a tiny part of it. We need evidence if she tries to play the innocent card. I'm sick and tired of witnessing men's inability to see the evil that lurks behind her pretty face. Seriously, enough is enough!"

"Welcome to my world!" Giovanna sighed dramatically, and Jessica grinned at her, amused.

She seemed like a nice and level-headed girl. Jessica had no idea how she managed that since her mom was clearly deranged.

"You know that I want to help, so whatever plan you have, don't you dare to leave me in the dark."

"Don't worry. I'll need all the help I can get to make my plan work. Now, if only you could give me Myra's cell phone number, that would be perfect."

Giovanna pursed her lips and slightly pouted after. "Well, about that... Myra and I didn't communicate through her new cell phone number. They could find out she was a spy because of it."

"So how did you talk to her?"

"We used an old spy trick. I was placed here in

America to communicate with her and support her in case of need. I was basically her handler."

Jessica frowned. "How will we contact her?"

"We'll need to leave her a message in the Boston Public Library. I'll write you the instructions. We can place a message with the number from your new burner phone, stating that it's urgent. She needs to break protocol and contact us. I'll pick up the call. She knows and trusts me."

The witch nodded, agreeing with her idea. "But where in the Public Library? That place is huge."

"I know. It was the only place we thought they wouldn't suspect anything since she's a witch, and witches tend to be surrounded by books. There are a lot of old and important documents there that she can access to gather information for new spells and incantations. We choose a specific book to contact each other. We circle letters in a specific page and leave secret messages to each other."

"Does she go there on a daily basis? How many times a week would you contact her?"

"Once a week. Normally, only to find out if she is okay."

"When will she go again?"

"Tomorrow, I hope." Giovanna bit her lip and ran her hand through her hair.

"So, I'll just go there tomorrow and wait for her so I can talk to her face to face."

"No," Giovanna said as she shook her head. "It's too dangerous. She can be followed."

"The library is huge. We need to talk to her as soon as possible. I'll sit there and wait for her. What section is the book in?"

"In the Main Reading Hall. But, it's too dangerous. You need to place a secret message in the book, today. Tomorrow, once she reads it, she'll phone us."

"And if she doesn't phone back?"

"Then we'll have to track her down."

"Do you know where she lives?"

"I used to know. She moves around a lot, depending on Vincent's orders. He's paranoid. We tried to track him to find out if he would go to Alaric's place, but we were never successful. He keeps changing cars in parking lots and using men who look like him to confuse us."

"Yes, he's a piece of work. If we have to leave a message in a book, we should get going. We have driven for hours, we haven't slept, and the clock is ticking. We should go to the library then buy supplies on our way back," Jessica said, looking at the time on her new cell phone.

"We could use some real food instead of the junk food we had to buy at the gas stations."

"New clothes wouldn't hurt either."

"And my mom?" Giovanna asked, getting up.

"She's out cold. She'll be out for a while, besides, even if she wakes up, she won't be able to leave." Jessica got up and went to grab her purse.

"We'll need to buy her blood bags. I know a supplier not too far from the library, unless you are planning to starve her to death."

"No, we'll feed her. Also, we need to have a reserve for you."

Jessica walked to the door but, then, paused as she faced Giovanna.

"What's wrong?" Giovanna asked.

"Giovanna, are you really okay with this? After all, she is your mom. Your dad will be extremely mad at us. He will become homicidal if he knows you have helped me."

"He will do nothing after he finds out she was planning to leave him and betray us to help Alaric. As long as nothing bad happens to her, I'll gladly help you."

"I'm not planning to get her killed or anything like that. However, we need to stop this insanity. Valentina's curse has killed too many witches and has endangered too many lives. And it is about time Alaric is stopped. Even if he was my son, he is evil. Marcus is right, we can't keep letting him get away with these deplorable actions. If no one else is strong enough to stop him, then, I guess, we girls have to team up and whoop his ass," she said, stealing a giggle from Giovanna.

"Just the two of us?" she asked. "I know you are bad-ass, but still."

Flipping her hair, she stated, "Nah, I've friends who will help."

* * *

It was nightfall when Jessica arrived at her new hideout with Giovanna. They were both tired and eager to eat and rest, but Jessica knew she wasn't going to be able to relax. Not yet.

"I'll check on my mom," Giovanna said, leaving the bags with new clothes on the dinner table.

"I'll take the food to the kitchen," Jessica warned, hugging the grocery bags.

Minutes later, they met in the living room.

"How is she?" Jessica asked.

"She's still out."

"Are you hungry? Do you want me to warm up some blood for you? Or cook something?"

"No, I'm good."

Jessica's phone rang, and she looked at the screen, opening the text message.

Giovanna asked, "All good?"

"Yes, my friend is almost here. She was alerting me. I'm just going to text her the number and the floor. I was taking precautions in case something happened and someone else read the messages."

"How do you know it's her?"

"Hum, that's a good point. But I've talked to her on the phone when you were paying for the clothes, and she seemed calm. She mentioned that she had some unexpected visits, so she was arriving a bit late. We were taking care of business, too, therefore, it's all good."

Giovanna nodded. "We took too long shopping for clothes."

"It was fun!" Jessica said, easing herself onto the couch. "By the way, thank you for paying for my stuff. I'll repay you once Anna brings me some money. I didn't have my wallet with me at the clinic and this hideout didn't have any money stashed away."

"Don't worry about it. It was my pleasure. And I'm glad Mom had money in her purse or Dad could have tracked us if I had used my credit card."

"Yes, I guess Valentina proved herself useful."

"Well, Mom always likes to travel with money. She likes to buy stuff but doesn't like Dad to see what she buys. Plus, they don't trust banks."

Jessica sighed, motioning for her to sit down. "I really need things to work out."

"You still haven't told me about your plan."

"I can only tell you once I talk to Myra and convince her to help us."

"She's scared. In the last message, she wanted to get out. I hope she calls. It has been two weeks since I left a message for her. I had been locked up and…I have no idea when was the last time she went to the library."

"Yes, that's troubling. Let's hope she's a good spy and follows protocol."

"She's just a scared kid," Giovanna whispered, sitting down and placing her hands between her knees. "I'm tired."

"You should go shower and then choose a bedroom to rest. I'll be here. You don't need to keep me company."

"I have no idea if I'll be able to sleep."

The conversation was interrupted by the bell ringing.

"Your friend must have arrived," Giovanna said.

"Yes, it must be her," Jessica agreed, going to the door and smiling at the screen. The camera was showing

Dulce in her skinny jeans and white tank. She let her in and ran downstairs to greet her with a smile.

"What the hell were you thinking?" she asked upon the sight of her, making Jessica lose her smile and roll her eyes at her. Dulce had her hands on her hips and a menacing glare on her face.

"Glad to see you, too!" The witch greeted with sarcasm and gave her a genuinely happy smile.

"The king is worried sick about you, Jessie!" she said with a strained voice.

Jessica lost her smile because behind her someone else showed up that she hadn't invited for her girls' power party. "Dulce, I told you to come alone!"

"And do you really think I wouldn't join you in whatever crazy plan you have?" Sebastien's voice was heard as he stopped next to his sister. The twins smiled at her as she scowled at them.

"Did you tell Marcus of my whereabouts?" she asked, growling at the twins with that frustrating thought.

"Of course not! We've got your back!" Sebastien retorted, seemingly offended by her question.

"Good! I don't want him to stop me."

Sebastien arched an eyebrow. "Stop you from doing what?"

"You will know soon enough!" Jessica grinned widely. "Now, group hug," she shrieked, excited for having both of them with her and jumping in their arms. She kissed their cheeks and ruffled Sebastien's hair, upsetting him and making Dulce laugh hard.

Then, they walked upstairs, so she could show them

her new headquarters, and they could greet their other teammate.

Moments later, they were all seated on the couches, ignoring the news on the muted TV and talking instead.

"I should be mad at you," Sebastien said, making Jessica look at him with puzzled eyes. "I can't believe you asked Dulce to come when we've know each other for so much longer. You kept me in the dark and didn't ask for my help. I thought we were best friends, Jessie!"

"Oh, stop pouting. You're a grown man for God's sake! I didn't know if you would tell Marcus or not. And, I didn't want my mate to get upset with you because of my temper tantrum."

"Are you are confessing that this is a tantrum, and you shouldn't have run away from the king?" he asked with a cocky smirk, making her look at him sideways.

"Well, I have the right to feel upset with him. You can't understand. You don't have a mate."

"Thank you for reminding me of that." He folded his arms and sneered at her.

Jessica just showed him her tongue and made him chuckle. But, she wasn't feeling happy anymore. "Is he missing me?" she asked, in a low voice as her eyes stared at her hands. She was trying to make her heartbeat slow down so she wouldn't show how she was actually feeling.

"No, of course not. He's moved on rather quickly and found himself a new mate. One that doesn't run away from him," he said.

Jessica glared at him, upset by his mean words.

"I'm sorry, but you were too hard on him this time."

"I'm coming back, after!" She sulked and stared at Dulce who was quiet with sympathetic eyes.

"Men never understand our reasons," she said and Jessica nodded to her and then stared at her twin brother with dejected eyes.

"Yes, blame it all on us," Sebastien sighed deeply. "Jessie, you know I'm right."

"Maybe, but you don't need to be this mean about it," she explained, knowing or, at least, hoping it was his awful attempt at a joke. "You are joking, right? He isn't…he still wants me back, doesn't he?" Her heart tugged in her chest as her breath became strained due to anxiety.

"I shouldn't be joking. The king didn't deserve you running away from him."

"Well, I didn't deserve to be treated like a helpless girl. Only to be tricked into losing my memories and having a seizure at what should have been a nice and pleasant dinner with my friends and family. He was not going to do anything about Valentina. She was planning to have me removed from my own body. She was doing everything to upset me and make me doubt my mate and my mate doubt me." She paused to breathe. "I wasn't going to let her do anything else to destroy our bond. I don't care that he thinks it is best for me, but I was not going to sit there and wait to have my memories removed from me just so I could become the sweet helpless mate he had before. I'm done running."

"Calm down," Sebastien pleaded and gave her his hand. "I'm not saying you aren't right, either. I'm just saying you need to think about what you have done and how it has affected the king."

"Have you come here just to try to make me change my mind or did you come to help?" she asked, frowning.

"I want to help you. There is no chance in hell that I'm going to let you go ahead with your dangerous plan without us being here to back you up. Nevertheless, Jessie, you should contact the king and tell him, at least, that you are okay. You ran away and left him behind, almost making him lose his sanity because he didn't know what happened to you. He didn't know if you were taken or if you had left the hospital on your own will."

"Does he think I was kidnapped?" she asked, breathless, nibbling her lip hard.

Sebastien confirmed, "He did! But the hospital security footage showed a very different story. A story he is now concealing from the other king who is threatening to start a war if his wife doesn't show up."

"I can fix that," Giovanna said, intervening in the conversation. "I can calm my dad down."

"King Francesco is really upset, and your mate is moving heaven and earth to find you, Jessie," Dulce added.

Jessie stared at her. "I didn't need to run away if he didn't believe Valentina's lies and... Why is everybody scolding me? I was the one who almost died!"

Dulce frowned at her. "Yes. But you disappeared and they have no idea of what's going on. Francesco wants his mate back, the king is looking for you, and everybody thinks Giovanna and Valentina were taken with you. Your mate is supporting the kidnapping idea, so you aren't blamed for Valentina's disappearance. But, I don't think that the truth can be hidden for much longer. Francesco will eventually find witnesses who saw his wife or his daughter. He will track her phone."

Giovanna grabbed her phone. "I'll text Dad, telling him not to worry about us. I'll pull the battery afterward."

"That will just raise more questions," Sebastien pointed out. "Plus, once you turn on your phone, they can track it to this location even if you disconnect it. It will always pinpoint the last place you used it at."

"Fine," Jessica muttered. "I have an idea that will calm everybody down. We've recorded Valentina's confession," she said. "I'm sure Dulce can lend me her phone, so I can upload the video and send it to Eric's email. Then Eric can show Marcus and Francesco the psycho bitch that Valentina is." Jessica shared her idea, waiting for feedback.

"Then Francesco will know that you have kidnapped his mate, and he will bring war to Marcus' doorstep," Sebastien retorted. "As much as I don't like the fact that you ran away from your mate, I like even less the idea of having Francesco putting a bounty on your pretty head."

"Well, I already have one." She shrugged, and he rolled his eyes. "Anyway, I don't think he will be upset with me," she said, smirking to cheer him up. "You have no idea what crazy plan that psycho had cooped up for her mate and me."

"I like Jessica's idea," Giovanna said. "I think it will calm them down for a bit and let us pursue Jessica's plan. Whatever that is."

"I like her plan, too," Dulce agreed. "If Jessica has a confession from Valentina, I think she should use it. We don't want a war. Plus, I can go somewhere far away from here to send the email to Eric."

"Hum. Let me watch that video to see if it's worth sending or not," Sebastien said, and Jessica nodded. "Come on, move your lazy butt off the couch and show me what you've been up to while I wasn't here," he urged her, making Jessica roll her eyes at his cocky alpha side.

"Please don't patronize me, sweetie," she retorted as she got up. "I have fire powers, and I'm not afraid to use them," she threatened with a wicked smile.

Sebastien grinned. "You also have cunning powers and an ability to put an entire community of supernatural beings to look for you."

"What can I say, I'm magnetic like that!"

"I just hope the king has a nice plan to ground you for being this sneaky."

"That would be the day!" Jessica growled, placing her hands on her hips. "I'm not playing, Sebastien, and I'm not a little kid who broke a window and ran away. Marcus and I will have a serious conversation when I'm done with my plan."

"Don't you miss him?" Sebastien asked in a low tone that made her stare at him. He was serious, matching her serious face.

"I do, but there are things I need to do that he wouldn't let me. I can't explain it, Sebastien. I need to do this, and he would try to stop me. I don't want to be stopped. Even if my heart is hurting, even if sometimes I feel like I'm going to burst into flames any moment now and scream until I run out of air and voice. I need to do this."

His hand rested on her shoulder as he looked at her with sympathetic eyes. "I'll keep you safe, Jessie. I'll help you. I like you a lot, and I want you to go back to your king and have a happy life. I love you as if you were my sister."

"Thank you, Sebastien," she said. His words brought some tears to her eyes, and she hugged him. "You are the sweetest guy, and I would love to have a brother like you."

"I would love to have a mate like you," he whispered.

She let him go and slapped his shoulder with teary eyes. "Shut up! Your mate will come when she is supposed to, and she will be how she needs to be. Okay? So stop saying nonsense and let's just watch the video. I haven't seen it yet. I have no idea if everything was fully recorded and if it's useful," she declared, wiping her eyes and taking a deep breath.

"I'll order food while you two are chatting," Dulce said, taking a hold of the menu that was on the table.

"Best idea ever! I'm starving, and I don't feel like

cooking," Jessica told her while walking with her brother to the room where the camera and the recording material were stored.

## CHAPTER FOUR — ALPHA DEREK

### KEVIN

Kevin entered the glass-walled office of his former boss' headquarters. Alpha Derek eased himself into the comfy office chair behind his nearly empty desk and motioned for Kevin to sit down across from him in the other leather chair.

"I'm afraid you have wasted your time coming here. I have no news about Jessica, and she didn't ask for my help," the Alpha said, scrubbing down his face and breathing harshly.

Kevin sat down and watched Derek's tired face with dark bags under his eyes. "What's going on? You look like shit!"

"Since your sister and her team quit on me, we are having a bit of trouble controlling some of the most violent factions. However, this week has been more stressful than ever. We are receiving news of riots in several big cities. My men are tired. I'm tired."

"You should go home and rest. See your beautiful daughter and just come back here tomorrow."

"I brought Amy to live in the compound. I was worried about her safety out in the community. Rogues have been targeting hybrids more than before. I'm looking for a new place to live. With a forest nearby, if possible. It's no longer safe to live close to the city with so many new packs trying to enlarge their territories, and rogues preying on smaller packs."

"My grandpa's little kingdom is a great place to live. There's plenty of space and the community is friendly."

Alpha Derek clasped his hands over his desk. "I'm looking to buy a farm or a ranch, but if he has land to sell…"

"I don't know about land, but there are plenty of houses available to rent in town."

"Werewolves live in communities. The pack wouldn't be happy living away from a safe place to shift and hunt."

"Well, the outskirt of Chicago isn't exactly safe."

"There are plenty of places with savannas, flatwoods, and forest to keep us happy. However, the attacks against hybrids are becoming insufferable, and the community is growing restless and mistrusting. There's an increase of packs being attacked. We are already swamped with the duty of protecting the humans against the supernatural threat. We can't afford a war with our own kind."

Kevin arched an eyebrow. "Why not? What are you afraid of?"

Alpha Derek reclined in his chair before he explained, "For starters, they attack families. They don't spare the children or the women. They exterminate entire packs because they want their territory. I spend most of my time here, so I can't be there to protect the pack. The majority of the males are here with me. Do you see my problem? Our families are left unprotected."

"Why haven't you reached out for help? I could have come."

He shrugged. "You have your own problems to deal with."

"Not really, it's been quite boring. My sister is in love and doesn't seem to be capable of letting go of her alpha mutt. No offense."

"None taken," Derek said, smirking at Kevin's scowl. "I know that you, *cats*, are just jealous of our amazing strength and witty personality."

"Yes, sure we are." Kevin rolled his eyes. "They seem to get along fine, though. So, I'm happy if she's happy." Kevin explained before resuming his need to vent. "And then, there's the fact that Jessica is my grandmother. She keeps my grandfather extremely busy, as you already know, due to my visit since I came here to try to find her."

The alpha smirked widely. "Yes. That must have been interesting since you had a huge crush on her."

"Well, she's freaking hot and you can't say much, she had you wrapped around her little finger. That's why I need to ask you again. Are you sure she didn't ask you for help?"

"I'm pretty sure, Kevin. I haven't talked to Jessica since she went to Italy."

His shoulders slumped as he breathed out loudly. "Well, that sucks! I would call Jason to come and help us, but he's too busy chasing my cousin Sasha around London."

"Is he still dating the vampire princess?"

"Yes, though they break up a lot and then get back together. It's a love-hate kind of thing."

"I don't get that. I really don't have a lot of time to understand how relationships work since I have my daughter and my work to take care of."

"Any news about Amy's mother?" Kevin questioned, sitting straight. Amy was Derek's daughter.

Derek's face grew sadder. "Since she ran away with that biker fellow, the only time she calls is to ask for more money. She doesn't want to know about Amy. I have filed the papers for divorce. I should have done that two years ago, but I thought she would come to her senses or, at least, come back to see her daughter."

"She was never happy with her life. A human among us…it's always bad news."

Derek shrugged and stretched his arms. "I'm tired and hungry. I need to see my daughter, and I'm afraid you've wasted your time coming here."

"I didn't waste it. I still need the locations of the hideouts from New Haven, Boston, and New York. Plus, I know all of the safe houses are connected, so once a code is inserted you will get notified. I need to know if Jessica has activated any of the safe houses using her code."

"Winona can take care of that for you. You just need to go to the terminal and tell her that I gave you the authorization to access that information."

Kevin narrowed his eyes and leaned forward. "Where's Liam?"

"He had a family emergency this morning and had to

leave..." Derek pursed his lips and narrowed his eyes. "Yes, now that you've asked...it was rather strange. He doesn't normally leave like that, and he has been complaining about the lack of field work. In my defense, he is a lot more useful here with his computer, helping our field agents, than out in the field himself."

"The only thing that Liam loves more than computers is Jessica. I'm sure his family emergency was her. So, we are literally screwed if she has him with her. He would have erased her tracks by now, and he will know if someone tries to access her information from here."

Derek gripped his fingers over the edge of his desk. His thick eyebrows drew together into one as his lips straightened, forming a thin line. "What is Jessica planning to do that requires Liam's help?"

"Alaric has put a bounty on her head. I'm pretty sure she is going to use that to try and find his hideout."

Derek got up from his chair as if he had all the time in the world, but Kevin knew better. His hands pressing on the desk to push his body up were an indication that he was tense.

"I'll call Liam. Meanwhile, talk to Winona and see if Liam was careless. I'll assemble a team to go with you as soon as you know something about Jessica's location. She'll need our help, and I'm sure she isn't foolish enough to go on her own."

"Grandfather believes Anna will help her."

"Have you talked to your sister?"

"Not since this morning."

"Ask Winona to pull Anna's cell phone location. Her

movements may tell us where Jessica is."

"She's smarter than that. She won't leave a trail for us to follow."

"Did your grandfather do anything for Jessie to run away from him?" Derek asked after a few seconds.

"Not intentionally. She might have lost her recent memories. It's complicated. But grandfather loves her. He would never hurt her."

"I'm going to help and, after this mess is over, we will need to talk about your role on this strike team. I need men like you, Kevin. I may need a replacement to lead the agents in Chicago if I decide to move to another place."

"I'm always up for a new challenge. Plus, I have new Intel about my tattoo and the database here might be what I need to find more information about where the witch's relatives may live now."

"Let's go," Derek said, striding his way to the exit. "You can tell me all about that on our way to the computer lab."

"Aren't you calling it 'The Bridge' like Liam wanted to?" Kevin asked, following the Alpha.

"That's not going to happen. They kept saying, 'Captain on the bridge' every time I entered."

Kevin laughed. "I hope you know why they said that."

Derek's lips twisted up in a bored grimace. "I'm not that stupid, I have seen Star Trek movies plenty of times. I just didn't want to indulge them in their nerdy behavior. If I don't control them, they will soon be calling their computers 'my precious' and talking Klingon or Elvish among themselves!"

Kevin's laughter was heard along the corridor for a few seconds before Derek shoved him against the wall to shut him up.

* * *

## JESSICA

The next day went painfully slow. Jessica kept staring at her phone, waiting for Mara to call back. Meanwhile, her friends were trying to entertain themselves. She also managed to show Sebastien the footage she had recorded of the demented plan Valentina had in store for her mate and Alaric.

Jessica spent her day trying to watch movies and eating pizza while pushing away the fact she was failing to attend her own wedding and was running away from her soul-mate. Other than that, she was focused. She needed to be if she wanted to go back to Marcus.

"I still can't believe it." Sebastien broke the silence, tapping his fingers on the leather couch.

"What?" Jessica looked at him, eager to find something else to think about other than Marcus and how much she missed him.

"Her plans and her confession."

"Oh, that." Jessica shrugged as she looked at Giovanna. "Did Myra call?"

"Not in the last two minutes."

Arching an eyebrow, Sebastien asked, "What will we do if she doesn't call?"

"Eat more pizza," Jessica stated as she opened her mouth to bite a slice.

The Alpha rolled his eyes and got up, walking to the window on the opposite side of the room. "I'm bored."

"We can see that," Dulce said, reclining in her seat. "Have you talked to Kevin?"

"You didn't tell Kevin where I was, did you?" Jessica asked, frowning at Sebastien who had his back to her and his arm stretched against the window pane.

"He called. He's in Chicago looking for you, and I lied about where I was."

Before Jessica could say anything else, the doorbell rang, startling everybody.

Jessica knew it was Anna, so she went flying downstairs to get her, not even bothering to look at the screen. But, when she arrived outside, she growled when she saw Shane behind Anna's back. Against Jessica's request, her best friend had brought her soul-mate with her.

Crossing her arms, the witch muttered, "I don't recall sending an invitation with a plus one."

"You should know by now that where I go, he goes," Anna said with a cheeky smile.

Jessica gritted her teeth. "This was supposed to be an all-girls team! So much for my awesome plan."

"Chill," Anna said as she grabbed the door to enter. "No one followed us, no one knows where we are, and Shane isn't going to tell anyone."

Stepping back to let them in, Jessica mumbled, "You had better be right if you want me to keep being your best friend."

"We will need his help," she spoke softly.

Jessica sighed slowly and nodded in agreement, only to complain again. "Yet, he's Marcus number one. What makes you so sure?"

"I brought gifts," Shane spoke, showing her a bucket of ice-cream he had concealed behind his back.

The sight of ice-cream wiped off the worried expression on Jessica's face. She jumped with happiness and grabbed it. Then she walked past Anna and said, "Smart move." She climbed up the stairs and added, "You two can stay. I'll grab some spoons."

"You're welcome," Anna yelled at her.

"Whatever!" she shouted back. "Make yourselves at home. Grab a seat and eat some pizza."

Now that her elite crew was reunited, all she needed to do was wait for Myra to see the message and call her so the plan could be set in motion.

## CHAPTER FIVE—INSIDE HIS DREAMS

### MARCUS

The wind was making the delicate lace curtains softly dance under the moonlight. It was quiet and still outside as Marcus preferred when he had this dream. He was in his old bedroom—the one he slept with Isobel. At the present time, it was different from what it had been. However, he would often find himself there when he wanted to remember his dear wife and their magical first night.

In his dreams, Isobel would normally be there, waiting for him when he entered. She would jump into his arms and kiss him until he couldn't breathe, and his heart would beat so fast inside his chest that he would get dizzy with desire and love. It had been days since he returned to that place inside his dreams. Ever since Jessica appeared, he no longer needed to dream about his old memories. However, he was desperate and needed to see and talk to his soul-mate. She was not letting her guard down, so he could use their telepathic link. She was being stubborn and reckless! She would give him a heart attack someday.

He hoped to find her there or enter her dreams and talk to her. They dreamed the same things. They shared a bond even before they had found each other again. He was convinced his dreams with Isobel, in that bedroom, were Jessica and he meeting and sharing that memory together. But, she was not there to greet him that night. All was quiet and still as if Isobel's ghost was gone from his night and day dreams. As if Jessica was denying his calling and ignoring all they had lived and shared together.

*Why couldn't he dream with her anymore?* He wanted to see and feel her. Hold her close. He was hoping she would come there to their special place, so they could talk. They made a lot of promises. He needed Jessica back. He didn't care if she would come as Isobel or as Jessica. He loved them the same. Regardless of what Jessie thought, there was no doubt in his mind that she was his love, that she had been Isobel, and that his love for her was real. He loved her even more now. He worshiped the ground she walked on. *So why wouldn't she sleep and come to him?* He was calling for her, helplessly trying to guide her there.

Sighing, the king laid back on the bed, staring at the ceiling. Maybe she wasn't sleeping, or she was simply ignoring him. She could have better memories to dream of. Yet, in her diary, that part of their previous life was the one that she dreamed of the most. Maybe it was just a long shot, and Jessica wouldn't show up in that bedroom.

As his lonely thoughts consumed his mind, he heard the sound of footsteps, followed by the sound of a door closing. He got up and sped his way to the door that he opened.

Outside there was nothing more than endless dark passageways and no signs of his beloved.

His imagination was playing tricks on him.

Leaning back against the door, he closed his eyes in grief, aware that he was useless in summoning his mate. A new noise was heard, he opened his eyes and glanced at the corridor, noticing the paintings curling and distorting as if they were formable and immaterial.

That corridor was the exact replica of the second floor of his palace. It led to his library. The perpetual dimness around him reminded him of his own memories when he haunted the palace and imagined that Isobel was alive and waiting for him to go to her. It was always night when they met. He opened endless doors, searching for her. He followed her laughter and chased her ghost along the labyrinth-like palace that would gain extra corridors and endless staircases.

The sound of books falling and pages being turned caught his attention and stole him from his reverie.

Someone was in the library.

He headed there, but the hallway kept stretching and the library door seemed more unattainable with every step. He persevered and reached out for the doorknob. There was none. Splaying his hands against the cold wood, he tried to push it open. A cold sensation rippled down his back as if something evil was coming for him. He felt the air leave his lungs. His breathing hitched as if he were suffocating. Black fog swirled around his legs as he stepped back and looked around. There was something different about that dream.

Inhaling deeply, he tried to take control of the world he was in. He wanted to see Jessica. He was sure that if he wished hard enough, he would be able to summon her there.

He placed his open hands against the door and, this time, it opened with a loud creak. He stepped inside the almost empty library as he noticed a few shelves and the dimness of the section. The windows were dark as if a coat of black paint had been spread over the glass. The floor cracked with his steps, and the room looked abandoned as if time had taken a toll on that place. Years of neglect and dust had imprinted a look of desolation in that familiar place.

His attention was directed to the opposite side of the library when he heard books falling. There were shelves blocking his line of sight, but that sound meant someone was there.

"Jessie," he called, his voice almost inaudible.

He stepped forward, passing the shelves and seeing an old desk against the wall where Isobel's painting was half-covered by white paint. Stacks of old books were piled on the desk. In the corner of the room, he saw a shadowed figure seated in an old armchair and a cauldron where black smoke rose to the ceiling and disappeared. There were candles scattered over the piles of books. Ancient scrolls were neglected on the floor.

Grabbing a candle, he stepped closer to the figure in the shadow and saw Isobel's brunette version reading a book.

"Isobel!"

Before he could walk to her, he hit an invisible wall. The candle fell on the floor, and he stomped on it before it could cause a fire.

Splaying his hands on the invisible wall, he called again. "Jessie! Can you hear me?"

No reply. She didn't seem to be aware that he was there.

Isobel got up and headed to the shelves where she browsed for new books. A few more fell on the floor and she returned to her armchair where she sat and skimmed the pages, clearly searching for something specific.

Marcus called once more. "Isobel, can you hear me?"

With a closed fist, he hit the invisible wall. The sound resonated inside the library. "Jessica!" His scream seemed to shake the space they were in because he felt the vibration under his feet.

He stumbled once the wall disappeared, and Isobel raised her eyes to him.

Stepping forward, he kneeled before her and put his hands on her face. "Can you see me? Is this really you?"

She tilted her head as if she didn't recognize him. Her eyes were vacant and her face free of emotion.

"Do you know who I am?"

"I need to find it," she said as she pushed him away and showed him the book.

"Isobel, do you recognize me?"

"I don't have time for this, Marcus," she complained, trying to avoid his hands. "I need to get another book. This one is pointless."

He placed his hands on her shoulders and prevented her from getting up. He noticed the modern shirt and mini skirt she wore and the paleness in her eyes. "Look at me. Do you know you are dreaming?"

"The spell," she whispered. "I need to find the right book."

"Jessica?" Marcus questioned. Even if she looked like Isobel, the fact that she wore those clothes and talked about spells meant that she wasn't really Isobel.

"Please." She pushed him again. "I'm trying to understand this spell. I don't know what I'm doing wrong because it's not working," she said with watering eyes.

Marcus leaned back to give her space. "What isn't working, my love?"

Isobel's eyes focused on him as she explained, "I think I may have translated it wrong. So, I was consulting other books to see if there are other versions of this spell, but I can't find any."

"Why do you need the spell?" he asked, brushing her cheek with his fingers.

"I –" she stuttered, confusion spreading into her eyes. "I don't know."

"Do you know where you are?"

"In the library, reading the books, trying to learn the ingredients for a magical potion."

"Do you know who you are?"

"I'm…" Staring at him, her body trembled and her appearance shifted between Isobel's and Jessica's. "I'm…confused."

"Do you know we are inside a dream?"

"Yes, I think I know that. I think I do," she whispered, staring around and focusing on the books. She got up and circled him as she walked to the shelves. "I really need to figure out what went wrong with the potion. It's crucial that I find the right translation. I might have used the wrong herbs or a wrong word in the incantation. Everything will fall apart if I don't get this right."

"Are you Isobel or Jessica?" he asked, noticing how her appearance kept changing as she browsed the books and talked.

She stopped what she was doing and circled to face him. Her eyes became blue and her hair turned blonde, but her face was Isobel's. "Who do you want me to be?"

Marcus stepped closer and grabbed her by her arms. "I want you to be you. I don't care what form you take. You are my mate."

"You don't mean that," she said as her voice trembled with grief and her eyes shone with unshed tears. "You'd rather have her."

Marcus shook his head. "That's not true. I love you. I loved Isobel, you are also Isobel. But, I love you now, Jessie. I'm sorry if I made you think otherwise. I want you to come back home, honey."

"I can't. I have important things to do here."

"I've seen the video, Jessie," he announced. His mate stared into his eyes with trembling lips and heavy breathing. "I love you so much, honey. Don't do this to us. She is trying to break us apart. She is trying to make you doubt me."

"I know. But I'm scared, Marcus."

"Of what?"

"Of losing myself. I know you want Isobel back. She would please you better."

"There is nothing about you that I would like to change. You don't need to try to be Isobel," he whispered, caressing her face, watching how she kept shifting from Isobel's appearance to hers. "Isobel and you are the same person. You just have a new body."

"I don't have her memories."

"You don't need them."

"But you would like me better if I did."

"I wouldn't. I love you the same, probably even more now because my love only grows more and more when we are together. We have made new and amazing memories, haven't we?"

She nodded and bit her lower lip, resting her hands on his chest.

"Who do you want to be?"

"Jessica," she said as she took Jessica's form.

He grinned at the sight of her lovely face and sweet blue eyes.

"Are you real or are you just an illusion?" she asked.

"I'm real, at least, I think I am, but I don't even know if you are real or not. I would wish that you were my Jessica and not just a figment of my imagination."

"I miss you so much," she declared, using her finger to play with the collar of his shirt.

He brought her closer until the warmth of her body touched his.

"I can barely sleep because I am away from you. I like this dream and your words, but I'm afraid I might wake up and realize that you didn't actually mean anything you said."

"If we remember this when we wake up," Marcus explained while brushing her blonde hair away from her pretty reddened cheeks, "and we remember everything we said or, at least, some parts, then we can tell one another when we see each other again."

"Okay," she agreed.

"So why are you here, sweetie?" he questioned, eager to understand what was troubling her. Maybe he could find information about where she was and what she was doing.

"I needed to read the books," she explained as she looked at the shelves and then back at him. "What are you doing here?"

"I needed to see you," he replied, seizing her arm and preventing her from leaving his side. "I needed to talk to you. I needed to..." he didn't finish the sentence because he brushed his lips against her rosy ones.

The touch ignited his passion. He didn't want to talk anymore. He needed to kiss and hug her against him. He had missed her, and it didn't matter if it was just a dream. She felt real in his arms.

Jessica leaned back as she protested, "I need to concentrate on my task. You can't just raid my dreams and…Marcus."

He didn't want to hear her excuses. He tangled his tongue with hers, preventing her from talking as they walked to the desk behind them. He swiped the books of the top and seated Jessica as he wrapped her legs around his waist.

"I've missed you," he breathed against her mouth as he cupped her face and kissed her again.

She didn't resist him. Her hands tangled in his hair as her kiss became as hungry as his.

Catching her breath, she reasoned, "Marcus, you shouldn't be here tormenting me. I need to find something important. This is not the time to be having an erotic dream."

His smile brushed against her smooth and delicate lips. "I can't stop touching you. We can talk about what you need later."

Jessica's gaze endured his as she seemed to think about her next move. "But..."

"What do you need to know, honey?"

"I need to translate a word, but I can't find the spell in a different language to understand what I'm doing wrong."

Brushing his fingers against her face, he placed his forehead against hers as he caught his breath. "I can help you with that. You just need to tell me the word, and I'll give you the meaning."

"But—"

He placed his finger on her lips. "After you kiss me and make love to me."

Widening her eyes, she asked, "Here?"

"Right here," he answered, kissing her neck and leaving small bites along the way. "I was going crazy," he confessed, placing his hands on her cleavage and shredding to pieces the shirt she had on. She panted, trying to grab his hands, but he didn't have time to open all those buttons. He wanted her right there.

"Marcus, you are being…"

She didn't finish her sentence because he kissed her feverishly while his hand moved over her breasts, and their hips ground together.

He felt her arousal against his own. She felt warm. His fingers drew circles on her stomach before his hands rolled her skirt up her legs and his fingers brushed against the fabric of her panties.

She didn't say another word. Instead, she gasped and used her hands to unbuckle his belt and take his shirt off. He helped her, and both removed the clothes that were preventing them from feeling each other's skin.

"Do you wish for me to stop now?" he teased in her ear, nibbling her earlobe and placing kisses down her cleavage and breasts.

She growled, upset, holding his head and forcing him to kiss her lips, tangling her tongue with his.

His hands covered her breasts and molded to them. "Shall I stop?"

"This is my dream, isn't it? So, I'll tell you what I want and how I want it."

He smirked against her mouth.

She nibbled his lower lip, hurting him in the process, but he didn't complain. He grabbed her panties and lowered them down her legs. Then, he let his boxers roll down own his legs, feeling peace fall over him when his cock found its way into her molten core. She moved against him, accepting him inside as she begged him to go deeper.

Moving her hips to her own rhythm of need, she kept thrusting as he obeyed her pace. He secured her back with one hand as he caressed her breasts with his other. His mouth was on hers, unable to stop kissing her. It was perfect every time they made love, even if it was in a dream and on a desk. It felt real, and he was gasping in pleasure against her delicious body while she milked him inside.

"Tell me where you are, Jessica?" he asked, watching how she panted and responded eagerly to his touch. Watching her face while they were making love would always make his blood race faster and increase the amount of pleasure he was feeling. "Tell me, honey. Where are you? Let me go and get you," he pleaded, grabbing her butt with both hands and going deeper. She gasped louder and squeezed him tighter between her thighs. He lowered his head to lick her breasts as his hips lost control thrusting into hers. Each stroke was more mind-blowing than the last.

"Just stop talking, already," she grumbled, securing her hands behind her back.

Leaning back, she pushed her pelvis forward, so he could go deeper.

He growled in pleasure, his fangs coming out, and his eyes closing to concentrate on the movements of their hips together. He increased the speed, attentive to her breathing and her shrieks of pleasure.

They climaxed as their mouths locked in a hungry kiss.

Jessica's hand played with his hair as she caught her breath. She kissed his neck. "I really didn't want this to be just a dream. I wanted it to be real. I wanted to make love to you one last time before... I didn't want to leave you. I swear I didn't. I love you with all my heart. And if I die, and we don't get the chance to be happy in this life, just promise me you will wait for me to be reborn again," she whispered in his ear.

Her words saddened him. "Don't say that. I will die if you are gone. I can't stand to live without you anymore. I want to be with you, and I want to love you. Just tell me where you are," he pleaded, tears watering his eyes.

He held her possessively, wanting to keep her there. If only he could keep her in his dreams with him forever.

"I can't," she declared, kissing his cheeks and forehead.

Her tears fell upon his face. There was nothing he could say or do to make her tell him where she was. She was a stubborn witch.

"You are killing me, Jessie," he complained, pain tightening his heart. "You can't leave me alone. You can't die. I forbid you."

"I don't want to die, but we need to stop him," she explained as her hands cupped his face, and she stared deeply into his eyes. "I knew you wouldn't let me do this if I was with you. You think I'm helpless and can't take care of myself."

"I don't think that."

"You need to let me be myself. I have powers. I'm smart enough to take care of myself. I did well before I found you."

"I know... It's just... I don't want you to die again."

Nodding, she laid her head on his shoulder. "I know."

"What are we going to do?" Marcus rubbed her back and caressed her thighs, his body burning for more.

"Besides getting dressed?" she teased as she nibbled on his ear. "It's insane how real you feel in my arms."

"I don't want to let you go...yet," he complained, stepping back and letting her move from the desk and place her feet on the floor. "I'll make you regret leaving me," he whispered teasingly, turning her around as he spread her legs and took her from behind. She gasped, leaning forward as she secured her hands on the desk.

Marcus leaned over her back, speaking against her ear, "If you believe that this may be our last time, then, at least, we'll make it unforgettable."

His heart hurt from saying those words, yet his hips moved back and forth as his hands trailed a path around her until they cupped her breasts, and he pulled her against his chest. She didn't say anything else. She kept moaning and shuddering in his embrace as they made love again.

# CHAPTER SIX—DEALS, POTIONS, AND BABIES

## JESSICA

Jessica was feeling grumpy and moody that morning. Myra had arranged a meeting, even though she lacked the patience to listen to the girl's complaints and fears. It might have something to do with the fact that Jessica was only able to sleep for three hours the night before. Not to mention, she had the most erotic encounter with her mate while dreaming. It had been perfect, but it had also felt like a goodbye. She didn't feel ready to say goodbye to life or Marcus. Dying wasn't part of her plans and neither was having just the memory of a dream with her king to keep her company during the Eternal Sleep. To make things even more difficult, her dream had only made her feelings of the loss of him even stronger. She longed to see him, kiss him, touch him—really touch him—and tell him how much she loved him. Even if he was a stubborn and overprotective mate who thought he could rule over her.

Breaking his heart wasn't in her plans. She wished that the dream had been real, that he loved her as much as he said he did, that he wanted her for who she was now and not for what she had been in another life.

"Jessie, you're back! How did it go?" Anna asked, entering the living room.

Jessica stood motionless in the hallway, staring

blankly at the walls as her hands hung at her sides. Anna's voice snapped her out of her trance.

Blinking and turning to look at Anna, Jessica reported, "It went okay. I have their clothes if we need to use the illusion spell. Myra was reluctant at first. I offered her the money she needs to run away with her mate. She gave me Vincent's phone number, so I can move forward with the plan."

Arching an eyebrow as she rubbed her arm, her friend asked, "So, why the somber look?"

Jessica shrugged as she walked to the sofa and sat down, reclining back with an audible sigh. "It was difficult to persuade Myra to help us. She's terrified of being discovered."

Anna sat beside her and rubbed her temples with a worried expression. "Do you think she'll be a problem?"

"If she betrays us, she'll reveal she's a spy. Even if she's scared, I think she really wants to get out of there. We are the only ones who can provide her that opportunity."

"Hum."

Jessica turned her head to watch Anna as she rubbed her hands on her jeans. "Do you think my plan is ill-conceived?"

She shook her head. "Just risky."

Sighing, the witch massaged her temples as she complained, "I'm still missing an ingredient."

"About that...Kevin sent me a really peculiar message this morning."

Jessica frowned. "What do you mean? Do you think

he knows where we are?"

"No, nothing like that. He simply said that grandpa wanted you to know that the name of the herb is atropa belladonna. Did you send him a message asking him to translate it?"

"No..." Jessica sat up startled and fisted her hands as the information sank in. *Could it be possible that the dream wasn't really a dream? What if they had actually talked, kissed, and shared thoughts?*

"If you didn't tell your mate, how did he find out?"

Jessica looked at her best friend. "It's a really long story, and we don't have time for this now. I need to go out and buy the herb. I'll go inside and check on Liam, first." Jessica got up and smoothed her shirt down. "Has Valentina been fed today?"

"Yes, she's fine. But, you shouldn't bother Liam. He's kind of busy."

"Have you tested the tracking device he's working on?"

"Yes, we are testing it on Shane and Sebastien. We'll know more about it later when they come back."

"We really need it to work or we'll never find the location of Alaric's lair if we don't have a signal to lock on to."

Anna got up and walked around the sofa, only to grab the back of it. "We are also placing tracking devices on us."

"Myra and her mate are low-level soldiers. Using an illusion spell to assume Myra and Jake's appearance will be useless if we lose sight of Valentina."

"Yes, I know, but Liam is the best at what he does. And, he is positive about the validity of the device. Plus, I have good news. Liam has found the perfect isolated location to make the exchange," Anna announced, cheerful.

Jessica folded her arms with a serious face. "That's excellent, nonetheless Vincent might not accept it."

"You have to make sure he will. We are outnumbered, and we can't afford to get ambushed."

"Yes, I know," she said as she paced across the room. Then, she looked down the corridor with a hardened glare. "Where is everybody?"

"Shane is with Sebastien studying the place for the exchange while testing the tracking device. Shane also wants to place extra men on the top of the roofs around where the meeting will take place to prevent rogue shooters."

"Where are they going to find the men?"

"Sebastien is an Alpha. He has a lot of experienced fighters in his pack. He called Jerome, his beta. He is arriving tonight with twelve other men."

"That's good. And where are Dulce and Giovanna?"

"They went to get lunch. That brings me to another issue here. Are you sure we can trust Giovanna?"

Jessica shrugged. She wasn't' sure of anything anymore.

Anna pursed her lips and narrowed her eyes. "What is wrong with you? Are you having second thoughts about following through with the plan?"

"No, I'm just tired since I barely slept. I better go to

the kitchen and get things prepped and ready so when I receive the final ingredient, I can make the potion. Could you go out and buy the herb I need? It's a complicated potion and it will take a lot of time."

"Sure, no problem. How much do you need?"

"Whatever you can find," she declared.

"Okay. I'll just go and check on Liam before I leave."

Jessica nodded while Annabel entered one of the several rooms of the apartment.

Passing by to go to the kitchen, Jessica glimpsed Liam sitting at his computer desk, coding.

It was crucial to prepare the potions she was going to need. Everybody else was doing their part. She trusted them, and she believed they knew what they needed to do to make their plan work. Therefore, she needed to get her head back in the game. But, while she stirred the potion, her mind was far away, and remembering her dream.

Sighing deeply, she looked at her phone over the counter. She couldn't restore her mind link without Marcus invading her mind and figuring out all her plans and where she was. But, she could send him a text message...or call him. Just to listen to his voice. Yet, talking to him would break her and cause her to cry.

Against her better judgment, she turned on her phone, witnessing the amount of missed calls and text messages that had piled up. Marcus had left voice messages. She didn't have the heart to listen to his pleading and worries because she wouldn't be able to resist his request of her coming back home to him.

She also had an important call to make that day. She would strike a deal with Vincent—using the excuse of saving her own skin—and deliver the one guilty of Alaric's curse to them. In exchange for a lot of money, of course.

The money was for Myra, so she could run away and hide with her soul-mate, far away from that mess and sick spy games she had been forced to participate in. Myra agreed to help because of it. The girl wanted money, and Alaric was going to pay generously if he wanted his former witch lover to undo what she had done to him.

Jessica's fingers moved as if they had a mind of their own. When she noticed, her phone was already calling. Before she could tap stop, a voice was heard on the other side of the line.

"Jessie?" a relieved and sexy voice called as Jessica's heart stopped beating and her eyes watered. "Honey, are you alright?" Marcus' voice was emotional and tender. "I'm not mad at you, Jessie. I swear I'm not. Just talk to me. Please tell me you are okay."

Jessica felt a lump in her throat which prevented her from speaking. Swallowing hard, she finally got up the courage to reply. "I'm okay."

"Tell me where you are."

"I can't."

"Let me help you, Jessie. Tell me what you are planning to do."

"You have already helped me."

"I'm reading spell books after spell books to try to

understand why you need that herb. I'm going crazy over here. I would rather know what you plan to do, so I can help you."

"Did we actually talk last night while we were sleeping?"

"Do you remember it?"

"Yes..."

"Good! I hoped it had been real," he said. "Jessie, please, let me help you."

She sighed despondently as she bit her lower lip. Then, she said, "I've just called to thank you."

"Anna and Shane are missing. Sebastien and Dulce disappeared mysteriously. I know they are helping you with your plan to find Alaric. I'm your mate, Jessica. Why don't you let me help you?"

He seemed sad and really disappointed in her. Her heart shrunk in her chest as her eyes stung with unshed tears. It had been a mistake to call him.

Marcus spoke again, "I know you are scared. You think I don't love you, and I just want your old memories back so I can have Isobel. But, you are wrong. I love you even if you won't remember any of our past memories."

"You don't mean that," Jessica said as she walked to a chair and sat down, leaning against the kitchen's table.

"I mean it. Come back home."

"No."

He let out a sigh filled with anguish. "Why do you hurt me like this?"

Tears fell down Jessica's cheeks as she felt her soul shattering. She sobbed. "I don't want to hurt you, and I don't want to die. I want to live and have babies with you. But, I can't do that if you turn me into a vampire. You know that if I'm a vampire, having children won't be possible anymore. I will lose myself and my body will be occupied by your former wife and not by me. I know it will. And, I know you want me to change. I know that you'd rather have Isobel's memories inside my body and that it will only be possible if I become a vampire. But, I don't want to be a vampire, not yet. I won't live forever if I stay as a witch. I'm not immortal like you. I want to have my own family, my own memories. I want us to make new memories together. I want you to love me, just me," she blurted out all the agonizing thoughts and feelings that were heavy on her heart.

"You want to have babies?" he whispered. It seemed that he wasn't expecting that revelation, or maybe he believed it was a silly idea. *Why would he want any more kids when he had already had them with Isobel in a former life?*

"Why is that so strange? I want to have babies, and I want to have a family, but you have already had one."

"Jessie, Jessie," he called her name as if to calm her down. "Please don't cry."

Jessica sobbed even more with his request.

"Listen to me."

"I want to have a life with you, too. I don't want my life to be defined by things that happened in the past. I want to make my own decisions and live through everything again as something new and special…with you. But you'd rather linger on your past…" She wiped the tears from her eyes as she tried to calm herself and speak coherently.

"That's not true," he said. "You need to listen to me. Don't cry. It breaks my heart because I'm not there to comfort you, and I really don't want you to be alone right now. Just listen to me, okay?"

"I promise I'll go back home after I do this." She sniffled. "I miss you. Did you think I don't? I'll go home, even if you love her more than me, okay?"

"Do you mind listening to me?" he asked, speaking louder.

"Don't use your king's voice on me. I'm not afraid of you," she said, sulking.

"This is not my king's voice. This is a 'my-mate-is-stubborn' voice!"

Jessica hissed, upset by his words.

She heard him chuckling on the other end. "You are always adorable when you pout. Now stop being a hard-headed little witch and listen to me."

"I am listening."

"No, you are just babbling nonsense after nonsense."

"It's not nonsense!"

"Jessica, I love you with or without Isobel's memories. I want you by my side. I will be heartbroken if something bad happens to you. And, if you want babies, I want babies, too. I have no problem in starting a life with you and wait until you're ready before I turn you. Do you want a little witch girl for a start? You can stay a witch as long as you wish. I really don't mind, honey. I just want you to be happy. And, I'll do anything to make you happy. I promise you that. So stop crying, please, because there is no point in crying when I love you, and I want you more than anything in the world. We can have as many children as you wish."

Jessica sucked in a breath, trying to understand if she had really heard what he had said. *Was she imagining it?* "You aren't just saying that to trick me, are you?"

"Jessie, I know you don't know me well. We don't really have a history together, do we? Besides some past life dreams and some hot sex dreams when we are asleep. But, honey, you are my mate, with Isobel's memories or without. You are perfect, sexy, witty, and really smart. I can't see myself living without you. And You need to know that I don't lie and trick people, especially you."

Jessica squared her shoulder as she mulled over his words. "I know you have a kind heart. I also know that I'm your mate. You are not willing to let me do what I want, and you don't believe in my abilities. I'm not a helpless fragile woman. I'm a strong and powerful witch. I have the goddess' blood in my veins. I have survived until now. You need to stop underestimating me and start trusting my abilities and treating me as your equal."

"Okay," he agreed as she caught her breath.

Her voice trembled with the emotion. "Promise?"

"I promise, Jessica. Now, let me help you."

"Marcus," she whispered, dwelling on a thought that was tormenting her mind, "if I restore our mind link, would you know where I am?"

"If I try really hard, yes."

She reclined in the chair as she twisted a strand of

hair around her finger. "But how does it work?"

"I can see glimpses of what you see."

"But...is there any possibility of sensing my location like following a scent or an intuition?"

"I can see what you see, but if I don't know where you are. If I have never been there, it will be harder to track you quickly. Why Jessie?"

"I just wanted to make sure that if everything else fails, you could find me."

"It would be a lot easier if I knew where to start. Where are you?"

"In a big city."

"Don't be vague on purpose, Jessie, or I swear to the gods that I'll punish you when I find you."

"I would like to see you try," she muttered, upset by his words. "I'm not a kid anymore."

"Well, I was not planning to give you the same punishment that I would give to a kid."

Jessica arched an eyebrow, unsure of what he was implying. Then, she giggled. "You damn perv!"

"Watch your language, Jessie," he sighed, but she knew he was grinning. He spoke really sweetly after. "Tell me where you are."

Straightening up and walking to the stove, she said, "Tomorrow. I need to do something today, something really important. And, I need to call someone else for that, so I need to hang up now."

"Jessie," he pleaded, making her blood race and her stomach drop.

"Marcus, you said that you trusted me. So, you will

have to prove it."

"Okay."

She bit her lip, feeling warm and fuzzy with his words. "We will need a lot of men. Alaric probably has a lot of fighters at his hideout. So, we will need warriors. Can you assemble a small army?"

"Yes, I can do that."

"Good. Then I'll send you the coordinates tomorrow night. You can go from there to find and rescue me. Shane and Sebastien will be here to help you with that."

"What are you going to do?"

"Get myself into trouble, and I'll need a knight in shining armor to save me or, at least, help me escape." She tried to joke about it but knew he wouldn't find it funny.

"Okay. But Jessie, could you call me before you do that?"

"Why?"

"So I can tell you again how much I love you and so I can hear your voice."

"Okay," she agreed, smiling. "But, I have to go now. I love you, too. And I promise I'll be careful."

"Okay, baby. And please, reestablish our mind link the moment you let yourself get caught. Leave your mind open, so I see what you see."

"I can do that," she said, turning off the phone before she wasn't able to go on with her plan.

She had a witch to scare and a psychotic vampire to catch. She didn't need any more distractions that day.

## CHAPTER SEVEN — VARIABLES

## JESSICA

Jessica was pacing around her bedroom with her hands behind her back and her mind running through all of the possible scenarios, trying to figure out how she was going to save her awesome plan. Plans are great, but there are variables that can ruin even the most carefully constructed ones. She was trying to adjust and minimize the risks that those variables caused, so they didn't ruin everything she had meticulously thought out.

The door to her bedroom opened, and Dulce came in.

Frowning, the werewolf female asked, "What's wrong? Why are you pacing?"

The bedroom she was sharing with Dulce had two single beds. Jessica sat on the bed closer to the window before asking, "Where's Giovanna?"

Dulce combed her black hair as she sat on her own bed. "She's in the kitchen preparing dinner. Why do you look so worried?"

Jessica clasped her hands together and placed them between her knees as she bit her lower lip. "You will never guess what happened when I phoned Vincent."

Dulce leaned forward with a worried expression. "Did he refuse? Did he do something to Myra?"

"No. He never picked up because he's dead!"

Dulce's eyes widened. "How do you know he's dead?

Who killed him? What is going to happen now?"

Jessica motioned for her to slow down with the questions. "I know this because Alaric was the one who answered the phone. Imagine my surprise! I choked and, for a moment, I just stuttered like a crazy person."

"Who killed him?"

"Alaric didn't share that information. Whoever it was did the world a favor, but also messed with our plan. I tried to call Myra. I know I shouldn't. but I don't know if I can deal with the Devil himself on the phone."

"So, you are still planning to go forward with the plan?"

Jessica nodded. "I told him that I would call him later."

"Why do you think he'll pick up?"

"Well, I told him who I was and what I could offer him in return for leaving me alone."

"You told him that you had the original witch who cursed him?"

"Yes." Jessica bit her nail. "I didn't make any demands, though. I wanted to talk to someone else to know what I should do. Should we proceed with the original plan or come up with something completely different?"

"You should be asking Anna and the rest of the team, not just me." Dulce leaned back and placed the palms of her hands on the bed. "What did the big bad vampire tell you when you said who you were and what you had to offer him?"

"He seemed amused. Yet, I don't know if I can call

him again and try to sound friendly." Jessica sighed as she flipped her hair away from her shoulders and crossed her legs. "I just hope Vincent's death is something recent, and Myra is still alive."

"Alaric might not use them on the team to make the exchange."

"That too."

"Relying solely on the tracker... I don't know if that's such a good idea."

Jessica nodded. "That's also my fear. If the tracker doesn't work, we will lose the opportunity to find Alaric's hideout. We'll also lose Valentina. And, everything will be much worse if she undoes the binding spell, and he wins another powerful ally. She's crazy in love with that psycho vampire."

"She's not in love. She just wants to hurt her mate. She's deranged and needs help."

"Speaking of which, do you have news about the video you sent?" Jessica asked as she got up.

"I haven't checked my email since." Dulce got up and smoothed her clothes down. "I'll ask Liam to use his computer before we eat. Meanwhile, we should talk with everybody about what happened."

"Yes, I'm going to text Anna. She went out to buy an important herb. Sebastien and Shane are still scouting the industrial area for a perfect spot for the meeting. The other one wasn't viable."

* * *

After dinner, the girls reunited on the living room. Sitting on the couch between Anna and Dulce, Jessica dialed to talk to Alaric again. She turned on the loudspeaker so everybody could listen to what he had to say.

"Hello," Alaric's voice greeted her on the other end of the line. It had an edge of darkness that made her stomach clench and twist with fear. Jessica knew he was her son from another life, but all the harm and death he caused was enough to bypass that fact.

"Hi," Jessica replied, trying to sound cheerful.

"You took your sweet time to call me back. Are you ready to tell me what you want?" Alaric asked, going straight to the point.

"I have a deal for you."

"Yes, I'm quite intrigued about that. You claimed to have found the witch who has cursed me, and you will give her to me in return for a substantial monetary reward."

"Yes, that's right."

"But, don't you know that you are the only one that can break my curse? Didn't Myra tell you that when you two met?"

Jessica froze in a panic at his words. Yet, it was part of her plan to make Vincent believe she had looked for Myra in hope that she could help her in canceling the prize on her head. Maybe Myra was still playing accordingly to the first plan. Or maybe she had just spilled the beans, and Jessica's plan was ruined.

Alaric's mocking tone was heard, "Come on! Do you

really think that Myra wouldn't tell her master she had seen her cousin and that her cousin wanted to strike a deal with me? You have little faith in the blind obedience my subjects have for me. I have to confess, I'm extremely intrigued."

Jessica arched an eyebrow. "About what?"

"Why do you need money if you are going to get married to my old man? What is up with that anyway? Did you cast a spell on him? I saw the pics. You were walking in town extremely friendly. And then, I heard about the marriage! Do you really have some kind of a death wish? Did you really think I wasn't going to cook up a plan to have you kidnapped before you could fill my mother's shoes?"

"Well..." Jessica breathed in slowly as Dulce squeezed her hand in hers. "I really don't care about what you think about that matter. I'm calling you about a ransom, not to discuss your mommy issues."

"Hum. About that, I'm a bit confused how you can collect a ransom on your own head. Or do you think that I will simply pay you for your trouble?"

Jessica smirked. "I don't know, will you?"

His harsh voice echoed on the phone. "I can find you, witch. Don't play games with me!"

Jessica sighed, sounding bored as she rolled her eyes. She raised the phone closer to her mouth. "Darling, if you could find me, then you wouldn't be picking up the phone to talk to me. And, don't even bother in trying to find where I am. This phone number is untraceable."

"You are a clever witch," he said after a moment.

Jessica felt cold shivers of darkness curl around her heart. He was creepy, and he was a rollercoaster of moods. One moment he was sarcastic and the other he was mad.

After a moment of silence, Alaric asked, "How did you convince my old man that you were my mom's reincarnation?"

Jessica bit down her lip before she could gasp at his question. She looked at Anna and then at Dulce with widened eyes. *How did he know that?* He was too well-informed for someone who was supposed to be out of reach.

Jessica said with what she hoped to be a calm voice. "I see you have spies in your father's kingdom."

"Yes, I like to know how the old man is doing."

"He's not an old man," Jessica muttered unable to conceal her annoyance.

"He must be senile by now if he believed your lies."

Jessica clenched her jaw. "Have you ever stopped to think that maybe its true?"

He snorted. "Sure and maybe pigs can fly."

"They can if I cast a spell on them," Jessica informed him, not trying to be funny, yet that simply rolled out of my mouth. Alaric laughed nevertheless, but she didn't. His laughter frightened her deeply.

His voice echoed again with an edge of darkness. "You are intriguing and extremely good-looking. I guess that and your talent for the dark craft made it possible for my idiot of a father to believe your bullshit. Either way, I was not going to let that slide easily. If you hadn't run away, you would be right here with me, having this conversation face to face. And, trust me, to get what I want, I can be rather persuasive."

"I don't need you to tell me that. In any case, I'm the one with the leverage here. So, if you are through with the chit-chat and your mommy issues, can we negotiate now?" Jessica asked, annoyed by his cocky words and his stupid threats. "I should have spanked you harder when you were a kid, then you would have shown some respect!"

"Bitch," he snarled like a wild animal. "My mother was an angel. She never laid a hand on me!"

"That explains a lot."

"Fuck you!"

"I'd rather not right now. We have business to take care of," she said patiently, smiling to dissipate the wrath she was feeling for him. "But if you want me to call you later or never call you again, that's fine by me."

He growled into the phone, and Jessica heard something being broken. Then, she heard whimpering, and Jessica could only guess that the jerk was hurting someone next to him. A girl's voice, with a soothing tone to calm him down, was heard in the background. It worked because the growls eventually stopped. She had no idea of what was happening on the other end of the line, but it was probably some twisted stuff.

Moments after, he asked, "How can I help you?"

Jessica indulged him. "I think we are both pursuing the same thing."

"And what is that?"

"Revenge."

"I'm listening."

"The witch who cast that curse on you, and the one who kept me locked up when I was younger, is the same person. When I understood that she was the cause of my parents' death, I thought I should have my revenge and make some money in return."

"Valentina is long since gone," Alaric muttered. He clearly remembered the name of his former witch lover. "Don't try to trick me."

"I'm not. It's quite simple actually. Because she was a witch, you thought she died. However, what happened was that she was turned into a vampire and she is still alive."

"That's impossible. I have been looking for her all this time. Do you think I hadn't thought about that? I have even thought of the probability that she could have used dark magic to live longer. No one has ever encountered her and no one in her bloodline knew about her."

"Well, that is because she was well-guarded, and she had a strong coven protecting her from the other witches and wizards you have used to look for her."

Alaric asked with an apparent wounded pride. "And how were you able to succeed where I've failed?"

"She took me away from my parents and raised me."

"Why?"

"Personal matter. But, the thing here is that you need one of us to break your spell since you killed the rest of our bloodline in your crazy pursuit for a cure—"

"Where was she hidden?"

"With her mate."

Silence on the other end until he said, "You are the last of your kind and the strongest from what I've been told. What makes you think that I'm going to believe what you are saying?"

"I have proof. Besides, what is it worth to you if you have me or any other witch but not the right spell to break your curse?"

"I have a copy."

"Intriguing," Jessica stated. She had a feeling it would be a long conversation. "She didn't want to give it to me. I suppose that will make things easier for us when we discuss how much she is worth to you."

"Let me see if I understand what you want. You want to save your skin and, in return, you give me the one responsible for cursing me?"

"You are a smart guy, but again all of our family is," she said.

"You are not my family. You are not my mom. My mom is dead. I don't care what kind of bullshit you have said to the king, I'm not falling for your lies."

Jessica rolled her eyes. "Whatever, I'm not really looking forward to a family reunion with you. Let's not forget the fact you killed me, you prick," she accused him, annoyed by his stupid accusations.

He shut up for a while.

Jessica furrowed her eyebrows. He may have been offended, or he was just an idiot and was smiling wickedly at his past actions.

"It was an accident," he muttered. Then a smashing

sound was heard. "If you were truly my mom, you would know that."

Jessica recoiled in her seat. *What was up with all that violence?* He really needed to control his temper.

"Well, I can't remember it. I just have dreams about it. The fact is that there isn't a lot of hope of forgiveness for you, is there? You are a cold hearted vampire who killed your mom and sister and then, not satisfied with just that, killed your older brother, his wife, and tried to kill your niece and nephew. I would advise you to go see a psychiatrist, but you are beyond repair."

"Don't be a smart-ass, witch," he growled. "George married a panther. It was against the law. They shouldn't have procreated. And you shouldn't pretend that you are my mom's reincarnation. I don't care what you want. I want you out of my family's life."

"Well, don't worry about that. Once you give me my money, I'll be long gone."

Alaric breathed deeply before asking, "So, all this is because of money, is it?"

Jessica mustered all the courage she could to reply to him. "What else could it be? Did you think I wanted a family reunion with you?"

"How much do you want?"

"How much is Valentina worth to you?"

"I need proof that you have her."

"I can send you a picture."

"Pictures can be forged."

"I'll send you a video with her confession about her crazy plan to make you her soul-mate and bind your two souls together. I might say, you actually would be good together. You are both maniacal and self-centered."

"You are rather cocky, aren't you?" he asked, even though she didn't think he was actually waiting for an answer.

Jessica sighed with annoyance. "Think about a price and then call me when you have received my video on your phone. Talk to you later."

With a smile, she hung up.

Jessica tried to relax her tense body as she placed the phone on her lap and looked at Anna's face. She had been grimacing in despair at Jessica's evasive comments and cocky talk. "What?"

Anna sighed. "You pushed your luck."

Jessica shrugged. "It worked, didn't it? Alaric is a prick who doesn't like to be defied. He would only take me serious if I acted cocky. Plus, now he wants to punish me for outsmarting him. I'm counting on his arrogance to have a face to face with him."

"He's not going to show up. He'll send someone else," Anna said.

"Maybe, but he wants to break his curse, and he hates Valentina. He'll pay."

"Or try to kill us at the drop point," Dulce said.

"That too!" Jessica agreed.

Liam walked into the living room with his laptop in his hand as he looked at the screen. "The video is ready to be sent," he warned. "I've just uploaded it to your mobile."

"Thank you," Jessica called to him as she looked at

her phone and composed the message to send the small video with Valentina's twisted confession about her love for Alaric. He didn't need to hear everything, just the part that concerned him and the curse.

One minute later, Jessica hit send.

"Do you think he will believe it?" Anna asked, shattering the silence.

Jessica replied, "We'll find out in five minutes. I said what was needed to spike his interest."

Anna entwined her hands on her lap as she pursed her lips. "I'm just nervous, that's all."

"Everything will be fine."

"We have a spy in our midst," she whispered.

Jessica nodded and added, "Well, not on our team, but there is someone in the town or even in the palace, giving information to Alaric. If it was someone really close, he would already know about Valentina, and he doesn't. He mentioned some pictures. Maybe he had some detectives or bounty hunters in town."

"Even so, we should tell the king. If he is coming to help us, Alaric could be warned if he assembles a group of men to come to the city," Dulce reasoned.

Jessica turned to Anna's side. "You should text him."

"That's a good idea," she declared, reaching for her phone.

"You can tell him that we are all okay," Jessica added.

Anna said as she typed the message, "I don't think we will be able to meet him tomorrow night. We may need a bit more time if he doesn't accept your terms. Plus, make no mistake, Alaric will want you *and* Valentina. He's annoyed by the fact that you are pretending to be his mom."

"I have a news flash for him, I don't care, and if I could, I would spank him hard. He is a worthless, spoiled brat and needs to be sent to his room to think about the wrong he has done."

"I think he is long past that," Anna stated as she looked at her friend.

The sound of the cell phone ringing startled everybody. It was Alaric calling.

"Yes," Jessica answered lazily.

"I'll give you five million in exchange for that bitch," Alaric said without any kind of hello or how have you been. His voice was serious.

Jessica let his words sink in for a moment. "Five million?"

He snapped, "Or I'll just find you, kill you, and get the witch myself. Five millions or no deal. It's already double of what I would give for your head."

"I guess you have a soft spot for her then," Jessica teased.

"Meet me at–"

"Hold on. I didn't say yes and, even if I do say it, I'll be the one to set the meeting. I don't trust you. I will talk to my friends, and we will text you our answer together with the coordinates of where our meeting to exchange gifts will occur."

"Gifts?" he asked. "You are a box of surprises."

"You have no idea," she declared. "Talk to you later, hon!"

Jessica hung up and stared at Anna who was frowning at her. "The plan is set in motion."

## CHAPTER EIGHT — PUNISHMENT

The moonlight glowed on the stone wall of the cell Beth was held in. During the day, small fragments of silver brazed her flesh, floating from the same wall that was now receiving the moonlight. It was just another way of torturing her for what she did. She had been physically punished during the day. Her back hurt. The whip's lashes were still showing. Her flesh didn't heal because she hadn't fed. The pain was excruciating each time the fragments of silver touched her wounds. She wished for a quick death, but she knew she wasn't going to have one. Alaric wasn't going to let her go that easily. Not even after she had killed Vincent.

Alaric was enraged when he found out. She didn't try to hide what she did, though. She wanted Alaric to know that it was her, the weak vampire girl, who he kept tormenting for years, had killed his right-hand man. She didn't regret it either. Vincent got what he deserved. There was no way in hell she was going to let that bastard hurt her sister.

Alaric wouldn't understand her reasons. He wouldn't believe her. Beth put forth no effort to conceal her actions. She surrendered, endured the punishment, and the interrogation. All she wanted was to die and was expecting him to kill her. God could be merciful with her, for once, and take her soul away from that beaten and weakened body of hers. But she was still alive, suffering and begging to all entities to take her away from that place, to free her from her captor, and give peace to her soul.

* * *

Alaric opened the dungeon's door, the ominous creak sending shivers of panic to the ones who were kept down there. He heard their whispers, smelling the human stench of his slaves and prisoners. He was in no mood to play with his captives or inflict any pain on them. He didn't want anything to do with any of the new blood slaves either. His mind was set on one person only.

The prince descended the curved staircase and followed the corridor to Beth's cell. His figure towered over the small space while he peeked in to stare at his prisoner. She was quiet as if she was asleep, her back turned to him. He could see the whip's slashes on her skin, her hands tightly pressed together in the handcuffs that lifted her in the air, refusing to let her rest.

The scene aroused and made him lust for her. Even beaten and dirty, she was beautiful. Her hair was falling messily about her shoulders and her clothes were torn to shreds. He could imagine her legs under her ragged skirt. She had beautiful legs. There was something about her that made his blood boil and his heart hurt inside his chest. He wanted to make her submit and obey him. What started as a twisted game to punish his own soul-mate became an obsession to him. Beth was everything his mate was not, and he craved her like the blood he needed to survive. As much as he tried, he couldn't break her, and he wasn't able to make her love him. At least, that was what he had thought until that night. Even if he sent her there to be beaten and tortured for what she did, he had no intentions of disposing of her. He needed her around. He just wanted to punish her to remind her that he was her master, and she shouldn't disobey or lie to him.

Alaric opened the door and approached the silent woman.

* * *

Beth closed her eyes harder and tried to conceal her fear. Maybe if he thought she was sleeping, he would go away.

She had no such luck.

"Why, Beth?" he asked huskily, next to her ear, overshadowing her body and placing his hands on her hips.

Beth shivered and protested when she felt his torso leaning closer to her wounded back.

"Why did you do this to me?"

*What?* It was the question that raced through her tired mind. *What was he asking? Was he crazy? Why bother answering that question?* Time after time, he proved that he was perverted, evil, and mad.

He kept talking. "If it had been someone else, I would have killed them in a heartbeat. But it was you. And I can't kill you. I need you. So tell me why you did this."

He smelled her hair, nuzzled his nose against her cheek, and waited for her to answer him. She said nothing. He pressed his cheek against hers, closing his eyes. His hands slowly pulled her skirt up showing her legs.

She whimpered, reacting to the fear of what he was going to do. She was vulnerable, and he was a sadist.

"Don't ignore me!" he yelled. "You've been ignoring me this entire day. Beating you isn't working. And I...don't want to see you suffering any longer."

She opened her eyes, confused by his words.

"I don't want to hurt you anymore. Beth, please talk to me."

She shook her head and kept her mouth firmly closed. He growled, hugging her by the waist, against him. She shrieked in pain, her wounds burning against the buttons and the fabric of his coat.

"I want to fuck you right here. You make my blood pump so fast. You have no idea how bad I want you," he mumbled, using one hand to caress her thighs, slowly making his way to the middle of her legs. "How long has it been since we fucked?"

"Please," she gasped, terrified. "Please don't do this."

"So you do speak," he mocked. "Does this remind you of the things I did to you when we first met?"

The darkness in his voice terrified her even more. She wanted to cry but had no more tears left. She just whimpered, panicking, trying to forget the days of rape and torture he was talking about. They weren't pleasant memories. He was a sick and twisted bastard. She wanted him gone. She wanted him dead.

"I hurt you back then," he said, breathless, playing with his fingers against her panties and getting even more aroused by her crying. "You feel hot in here. Didn't Vincent give you proper attention?"

"Please stop," she begged, her voice hoarse from screaming in pain. She moved her body to escape his hand. He drew her closer, and she felt his aroused member against her butt.

All she could hear was her crying. The rest was deathly silence. The other prisoners didn't want Alaric to give them attention or that he would even remember they were there.

"Stop fighting, it's pointless," he ordered against her cheek, licking it and smiling when his fingers slipped inside her panties. "Be nice, Beth. I'm going to pleasure you with foreplay. I know you like it when I do this."

"I don't!" Beth denied promptly, livid by his words.

The twisted bastard thought her body liked his touch. It didn't. She despised him. She hated him with all her heart, but she was unable to prevent the involuntary physical reactions that he got from her. He thought it would make her fall in love with him.

"Your body does," he teased, trailing kisses on her neck and running his fingers inside her pussy, making her spread her legs. "I've missed tasting you," he shared, making her sick to her stomach. She wanted to throw up, but she had nothing inside. "I promised you, I wouldn't hurt you again. But Beth, I can't take my hands off of you. And I'm not hurting you. For once, please, stop fighting me. You know that I can make you feel good."

"Leave me the fuck alone," she yelled, irate, moving her body so he would stop touching her.

It was torture enough when he raped her without any type of regret or care, it was even worse when he started to rape her. It wasn't an enjoyable orgasm. She didn't want to have one with him. She hated him, but her body felt differently when he touched her with tenderness and he took his time to make her come. Alaric found a new way to torture her, taking his pleasure in the fact that she would blame herself for having orgasms because of him. He had told her that he would make her like having sex with him. And he was true to his words. At least, in his mind, he thought that making her climax was the same as making her enjoy having sex with him.

"It hurts," she gasped, trying to ignore the movement of his fingers.

"What hurts?" he asked, voice laced with yearning.

"My hands, my back," she sighed in pain. "It hurts," she sobbed.

"Tell me why you killed Vincent, and I'll take you upstairs again."

"You know why," she cried. Her body quivered, chasing away any unwanted pleasure that he could give her.

"Fuck! Why can't I make you wet?" he asked, clearly annoyed, moving his fingers away and caressing his protuberance against her. Then, with a finger, he pulled on her panties and shred them.

Beth cried, even more, dreading what he was going to

do next, incapable of escaping.

* * *

Alaric bent down and stared at her naked figure. He growled, shuddering with anticipation.

"It's been how long, Beth? One month, two weeks since we fucked?" he asked, aware of the last time he got her alone and made her his.

Beth had protested, she had cried, and she had tried to get away from him. He had to fight her and take her by force. But it was worth it just to see the shock on her face when he made her come. After several orgasms, she was tamed and quiet as a mouse. He didn't know why she had to fight with him every time. He'd rather have her willingly. He dreamed of the day that she would ask him to fuck her. Nonetheless, he couldn't deny that he liked to fight her and force her to submit to his will. He liked when she begged for him to stop. But if he was taking his time to please her, the least she could do was to be obedient and try to please him back.

"Tell me the truth. You've missed me, haven't you?"

"I have not," she blurted out, standing up to him. "I hate you."

"You don't," he declared. "You are just too proud to admit that you want me."

Tensing her body, she yelled, "Fuck you! I hate you. I would rather jump off a cliff than fuck you or beg you for it."

"Are you trying to upset me, Beth?" he asked with a

deadly calm in his voice. He parted her legs with his
knee and opened his hands over her breasts. "I thought
we already had this conversation. I'm your master, and
I'll do what I want to your body. I want to fuck you, so I
will, and you'll beg me for it," he said, raising his voice
menacingly.

"I'd rather die. Just kill me already," she snarled. "I'm
sick of your twisted behavior. I'm sick of you and tired of
living. Just kill me!"

"I love you too much to kill you," he whispered,
placing his hand over her pussy, groping, and playing
with his fingers. "And you love me. That's why you
killed Vincent, so we could be together. You don't need
to lie anymore."

"You are crazy," she muttered as her body stiffened.
"Your reasoning is absurd!"

He ignored her words. "I should have never given
you to him. I shouldn't have listened to your sister. I
wanted you for myself. And you just love me, you didn't
love him. He was an idiot, and I didn't want him to touch
you anymore. You didn't love him, did you?"

"Please stop," she begged as she kept trying to evade
his fingers. "You are hurting me."

"Stop teasing me! I'm trying to have a conversation
with you. I'm opening up my heart to you," he
complained.

* * *

Beth was in no mood to play his game and find

meaning in his twisted words. She was in no mood to pretend to care and calm him down. So, she said nothing.

"Fucking whore, answer me!" he growled, grabbing her by the neck and squeezing it until she couldn't breathe.

Yet, she didn't try to fight him. She wanted him to kill her. If she died, even momentarily, she wouldn't have to endure his presence and his repulsive appetite for raping her.

She didn't die. He stopped before she could embrace the darkness. He hugged her, breathing fast against her neck, emitting some sort of sobbing. It puzzled Beth, but she wasn't that interested in asking him if he was crying. She was hurting, he was molesting her, and the last thing she needed was to have a crying psychopath hugging her.

"She called me," he whispered. Beth had no idea of what he was talking about. "She said I killed her. She thinks it was my fault," he whimpered, grabbing her harder.

She shrieked in pain.

"You are the only one who understands me."

Beth wanted to slap and kick him for his pretentious words. She didn't understand him. She hated him but pretended to understand so he wouldn't hurt her and her sister.

"Let me go," she requested, barely able to speak. Her throat hurt because of him.

"No," he denied, his voice with the edge of childish stubbornness in it.

"Why not?" she asked patiently, trying to honey her voice to please him.

"Because you'll run away from me, and I need you right now."

*Just her damn luck.* He needed her like a cat needed a mouse to play with when it was bored.

"But I'm tired and it hurts," she whispered, revealing the true pain she was feeling. "Please...master," she begged while thinking of every single way she could kill him if she was free. She could smack his head against the wall. She could try to snap his neck. It was a temporary death, not like the one she had given Vincent when she had cut off his head. But she couldn't kill Alaric. She had dreamed of it, she had plotted a million and one plans to kill him, but killing him meant she would kill her sister. And now that there was another factor in the equation, she couldn't kill him even if she was beginning to understand that her sister was becoming as twisted as her soul-mate.

"Then tell me why you killed Vincent," he demanded, caressing her neck with his lips. "Tell me, Beth, so we can be together."

"You are hurting me," she complained because he was rubbing himself against her, gripping her flesh too hard.

"Don't lie," he ordered darkly, grabbing her face and turning it to watch him. He plastered his lips against hers, rough and uncaring. He tried to slip his tongue inside her mouth while she tried to free her face and escape his mouth. She screamed when two of his fingers invaded her sex and his tongue slipped in. Her screams were muffled by his mouth.

"It's your fault if I hurt you," he said, releasing her face so his hand could unbuckle his belt.

"No, no," she begged, listening to the belt coming off. She knew what was going to happen next. He had done it to her too many times. "Please, I'll do anything you want." She felt the leather around her neck. Alaric pulled it tight, choking Beth. She fought to release her hands, for air, and to be able to verbalize words. Everything was pointless.

"Relax," he whispered in her ear. "There is no fun in fucking a corpse."

She closed her eyes and cursed her life. *Why am I fighting for survival anyway?* It was better for her to lose conscience.

It was instinct. She wanted to die but she always found herself fighting for her life. However, there wasn't anything left for her in the world. She had no reasons to keep living.

Alaric always knew when to stop before killing her, but even if he had stopped the choking, Beth wasn't reacting. Normally, she would fight him harder. Not this time. Fighting was pointless.

"Come on Beth, don't sulk now. Play with me," he begged, freeing his pants and stroking his staff against her butt.

No reply and no complaint. He snarled against her neck, making the decision of biting his wrist and placing it against Beth's mouth. She reacted immediately, opening her eyes wide and receiving all of his troubled thoughts inside her mind. His blood healed her body but sickened her mind. One thing was for sure, he had found the witch and things were going to get dangerous for the girl. There was another negative consequence of drinking his blood: her body was flooded with the raw lust he was feeling for her.

"You feel so wet now," he whispered, pleased.

Her hips moved involuntarily under his fingers. She sobbed when he nibbled her neck, replacing his finger with his cock inside of her as he pushed it deep and made her quiver with a wave of pain. He wasn't gentle. He pumped inside her, using his hands to move her up and down on him. Growling like an animal in heat.

She kept crying, numbing her thoughts, concentrating on the information that his blood gave her about the witch and his plans to trick her.

"I can't hold it any longer," he declared, moving faster and making her insides burn deeper.

Beth calmed herself, ignoring the burning sensation. She wasn't going to give in this time.

Soon enough, he climaxed, letting his cock jolt inside her core. "You always feel so damn good."

Beth ignored him.

"But I liked it better the other night when you were milking me with your spasms of pleasure. Do you remember that?"

Beth wished she didn't.

"Do you want me to make you feel like that again?" He didn't wait for her to speak. He placed kisses on the back of her neck, caressing her back and placing his hand on her butt. "I can be really good to you, Beth. Stop fighting me. You know I love you. We will be together. I've found the witch and, soon enough, she will bind my soul to yours, so we can be together. You'll be happy like that. I'll make you happy. You will love me even more."

Beth sobbed harder. She didn't want that. She wanted her own mate, not Alaric. The worst that could happen was him forcing her to love him with a binding spell.

"Marie, you, and I, the three of us together."

Widening her eyes as she choked on her sobs, she asked, "What?"

"I know you don't want her to die. I know I said that it would be just you and me, then I realized that I really don't need to choose. Both of you can be mine. Especially now," he whispered in her ear, caressing her arms.

Lifting her up to soften the weight of her body, he eventually pulled her up further and released her from the handcuffs. She collapsed, being held in his arms before she could hit the ground.

"Do you like my idea?"

"I don't understand," Beth whispered. She truly didn't. Her body and mind were exhausted. "You said you would kill me."

"Myra told me everything. You didn't want to tell me what happened, but she did," he said, sitting down with her in his arms.

She panicked, refusing the kisses he wanted to give her.

"Stop," he ordered, grabbing her face and smashing

his lips against hers. "Hush," he hissed, placing small kisses on her face. "Hush. You should have told me. Mates don't keep secrets from one another."

"You aren't my mate," she said, trying to be stern with her tone of voice.

"You will be. Then, you will stop fighting me, and you will like my kisses. You will beg me to make love to you."

"I would rather kill myself."

He chuckled. "I'll miss this. But you won't kill yourself. And we will have plenty of time after the spell to bond. You won't be able to live without me as your sister can't live without me. You won't kill yourself. You killed Vincent to protect Marie and the baby. You can't kill yourself if that means you will kill her and the baby. And you love the baby, don't you? The little baby that is inside your sister's womb."

Beth was staring at him with a puzzled look on her face. He was twisted but too smart for her own good. *He was right.* She would never kill herself if it meant she could kill the baby.

"Vincent was planning to betray me. Kill my wife and make you his soul-mate. But you love me not him. You killed him to protect me."

"Not you, the baby," Beth protested.

"I can give you a baby, too, after the spell. I can give you one. Do you want one? We will be a happy family."

Beth blinked, exasperated. Alaric was so messed-up that it was beyond scary.

"You said you didn't want the baby," Beth reminded

him. "That you were going to kill him," she sobbed, remembering his evil words and threats when he found out about Marie's pregnancy.

Beth kept looking in his eyes, they were green without a trace of the monster, yet the creep had raped her and was torturing her, convinced that she loved and wanted him. She didn't know what else she could say or do to make him understand that he was mad.

"You begged me to reconsider," he reminded her.

"And you said you didn't want a son."

"It wasn't yours," he explained.

She closed her eyes momentarily, so she wouldn't lose her patience and scream at him.

"I'll give you one. Those stupid science tests that Vincent made you endure will end. We can have a baby after the bond is created. Would that make you happy?"

"I don't know," she mumbled, nausea taking over her.

"Does it still hurt?" he asked, with a soft voice as if he actually cared.

"What do you care if it hurts or not?" she snapped at him.

"Of course, I care. I love you." He hugged her closer, and she shivered in fear.

Displays of affection were rare and confusing coming from Alaric. If anything, it just made her even more afraid of what he could do next. "You are the only one who understands me."

She quivered, thinking of a way to kill him so she could stop listening to his twisted speech.

He trailed kisses on her face, looking for her mouth, tasting the dried blood and the salty tears.

"I'll take you upstairs to your bedroom. I'll wash you and take good care of you. Would you like that?"

"I'm tired," she answered, hoping he would change his mind and leave her alone.

"I know, but I don't want to be alone. I'll be good. I promise," he said, getting up with her in his arms, bridal style, and leaving the holding cell.

Beth sighed, knowing he wouldn't accept 'no' for an answer. She had to let him do whatever he wanted and stay quiet and pretend. At least, until she could think of a plan to get away from him and prevent him from using the witch to bond her soul to his.

# CHAPTER NINE—POTIONS, TRACKERS, AND TRICKS

## JESSICA

"This is how it's going to happen," Jessie said, in the middle of the living room with her crew surrounding her. "Shane and Anna are going to go disguised as Myra and her vampire lover. They will be their replacements, allowing us to follow Valentina to Alaric's hideout. I'll go as myself to the location where the exchange will be made and negotiate with the person Alaric sends. Sebastien and Dulce will have my back and make sure they don't try to kidnap me and break the deal."

"Which they most certainly will," Anna stated with a hardened look on her face.

"Yes, but we have that covered, too, don't we?" Jessica asked her with a grin on her face.

Anna nodded and winked at her. "Once I'm inside, we'll study the compound and open the doors to let the others come in."

"My pack will be the backup," Sebastien interjected. "And I'll contact the king with the coordinates to Alaric's hideout. I'm sure he'll be heavily guarded."

"It won't be easy," Shane said. "But the most important thing is to grab Alaric."

"You mean kill him," Sebastien corrected.

Everybody looked at Anna, waiting for her to say

something.

"First, we need to grab him so Jessica can unbind his soul from his mate," Anna explained. "I'm as eager as any of you to have his head, but Jessica and I agreed that we won't kill an innocent."

"She's his mate, she will want revenge," Sebastien stated.

"Maybe, but we can't kill a girl without knowing if she's guilty of anything other than being Alaric's soul-mate," Jessica explained, calmly. "He wasn't always evil. It was the blood thirst that did this to him."

"But he still needs to be put down," Sebastien declared.

Anna put a hand on his shoulder to calm him down. "We know. Trust me, no one wants him as dead as I do. He killed my parents."

"I'm not trying to be heartless about this situation," Sebastien explained. "I'm just afraid that our attempt to capture him alive will increase the body count."

"All you need to do is let me have him," Anna stated with cold eyes and a serious face.

"Let *us* have him," Shane rephrased her sentence as he snaked his arm around her waist and brought her closer to him. "I'm not going to let you out of my sight. We are together in this, and you aren't going to do this alone."

"Yes, we will have him. I'm sorry, honey. It was just a figure of speech," Anna said. "We are in this together."

Jessica grinned at them for being so cute together. Then, she added, "We are all in this together. Our priority is to grab Alaric, but we need to deal with his men to get to him. Sebastien and Dulce will lead the assault team to Alaric's hideout, and I'll team up with Anna and Shane to find Valentina since it's the most likely place to find Alaric. I'm sure he'll be eager to have a nice chat with the witch."

"And what will Giovanna do?" Dulce questioned.

Everybody looked at the quiet girl, who blushed as she raised her eyes to watch them.

"I have the perfect job for her, don't worry," Jessica smirked mischievously.

\* \* \*

A few hours later, the plan was set in motion. The night had fallen, and they were parked in the middle of a road in a dark part of an abandoned industrial area.

Patiently, they waited for Alaric's representative to join them in that isolated area, so they could make the exchange. It wasn't going to be easy. Jessica and her crew had to have eyes and ears everywhere. Alaric was most certainly up to something, and Jessica was sure he wouldn't miss a chance of grabbing her, too, just because she had the nerve to claim to be his reincarnated mother and Marcus' bride.

Therefore, it came as a surprise when Alaric's men arrived in two black SUVs, exchanged a few necessary words, delivered the money, and grabbed Valentina with her head covered. The vampire only asked Jessica twice if she was sure the woman was who their master was expecting.

Jessica confirmed, and Alaric's bully threatened her with being chased and found if she was lying. Then, the huge vampire, dressed in leather, walked to the SUV, carrying Valentina.

Jessica got a glimpse of Myra and her vampire mate in the second SUV, unsure how they were going to be able to exchange places if they were part of the crew in the SUVs. They were supposed to meet elsewhere to be replaced, not there.

Moments after the exchange, as fast as they had arrived, the SUVs left with a trail of dust behind.

"Check the briefcase. They must have placed a tracker inside. They were too quick with giving us the money," Jessica ordered Dulce who had been there to accompany the exchange.

"Liam," Dulce called in her earpiece communicator. "Do you have a device to detect trackers?"

"Yes, I'll be there in a moment," the werewolf said.

"Okay, please hurry. We need to make sure we aren't being followed home."

"How's our tracker working, Liam?" Jessica asked.

"It's working fine, but they have stopped a few miles ahead."

"They are probably searching for trackers like we are."

"Not everything worked according to plan," Liam announced.

"Yes, I know. Anna, are you there?"

"Yes, we're here. We'll follow the SUVs."

Jessica advised, "Keep your distance. I'm sure they left people behind to see if they're being followed."

"I'll take another route to get to them," Anna said into her com.

"The plan to replace Myra is still on. If she's able to leave the time and arrive at the checkpoint, you have a go to drink the potion and take her place."

"Okay, I'll be waiting for news."

"Nothing here yet," Sebastien's voice interrupted their conversation. "Maybe she won't be able to escape."

Anna declared with a sigh, "If not, we will take her place inside Alaric's lair. It will save us time."

"It would be better if you were part of Alaric's crew and entered his lair without raising suspicion," Sebastien said.

"We'll work with what we got," Anna replied.

"Okay. Good! Keep me posted," Jessica requested.

"What are you going to do, Jessie?" Anna asked.

"I'm going to get back to the apartment and gather the rest of the team to meet you where you're going. Wherever that is."

"And if they don't take Valentina to his lair?" Anna questioned the feared outcome.

"He's too eager to have her. Even if he's not taking her to his hideaway, I'm sure that he'll come to her. When he does, we'll be there, waiting for him."

"Communications off for the time being. I'll keep you posted if anything changes or it's relevant," Anna said.

"Good luck," Jessica said, turning off her earpiece communicator.

Meanwhile, a car had arrived, and Liam came out with a device that he hovered over the bags with the money.

Jessica folded her arms. When he kneeled and put the device on the floor, she asked, "What's the verdict, Liam?"

"Two trackers, one in the suitcase and other in the bills," Liam said, searching and finding two small chips.

"Destroy them, place the money in a new bag and give it to Dulce. We are still keeping our word, and you'll wait for Myra in the designated location."

Liam got up and cleaned his hands on his trousers. "And if it's a trap?"

Jessica looked at Dulce before stating, "Dulce is taking four of her best men, but you can go with her if you think you can help."

"I'm better needed at my computer. No offense, Dulce, but someone needs to access the traffic cameras and hack into Alaric's compound once we find it. We need to tap into all the surveillance cameras and turn off any silent alarms."

"No hard feelings. I'll see you back at the apartment," Dulce said, kneeling and shoving the money into a black gym bag.

Moments later, she left in a black SUV along with her backup.

Jessica grabbed the briefcase and threw it into a pile of garbage on the side of the road. Then, she walked to Liam's car and signaled the other men to enter their own vehicles.

"Let's get back to the apartment." Jessica sat in the driver seat.

Liam joined her and turned his laptop on.

She peeked at the screen. "Are they moving again?"

"Yes, they are traveling East, leaving town."

"Did they find the fake tracker we planted on her?"

"Yes. They were clever, they didn't destroy the two of them only one. The SUVs must have separated, because the remaining fake tracker is going West, into town."

Jessica's nails tapped against the wheel. "They think they can fool us into believing that they're taking Valentina to some other place while they are actually going in the opposite direction. Interesting."

Liam looked at her. "Myra is in one of the trucks. Maybe she will be able to get away."

"If she does, Anna and Shane will have the green light to change into them, but...there is also the problem that if Myra is going in the opposite direction, she can't be seen at Alaric's place. It will raise suspicions."

"True," Liam agreed as he typed on his keyboard.

Jessica sighed. "Well, if camouflage won't work, then we'll take it by force. You are the right guy for the job. You'll have to use your hacker techniques to blind our enemy, so we can save the prisoner and kill Alaric."

"They'll never know what hit them," Liam said with a presumptuous smirk on his face.

Jessica patted his shoulder and started the car. "We need to change cars and get the rest of the weapons. It's not going to be easy."

"I know, but we are ready, and we'll have more

backup soon enough."

## CHAPTER TEN—THE REAL PLAN

### MARCUS

The living room felt stifled since Marcus had entered the apartment that was Jessica's hiding place. The king clenched his jaw and sighed as he looked at Eric, sitting on the couch. He seemed to be exchanging text messages with someone. Meanwhile, Francesco, who had joined them, seemed as impatient as the king.

He heard movement on the staircase. Someone was arriving and, as if on cue, Jessica entered the apartment with a male following her.

"They are still circling, probably afraid we might be following them," Liam said as Jessica stopped in her tracks, and the werewolf with the computer bumped into her back. "What's going on?" He raised his head from his screen. "What the hell!"

"Calm down," Jessie said, turning back and placing a hand on his arm. "They're friendly."

Eric got up from the sofa. "It's about time you arrived. We were worried sick."

The king raised his hand and signaled for him to be still as he narrowed his eyes on the girl. "Who the hell are you and where's Jessica?"

"Where's my wife?" Francesco asked, lunging forward. Marcus grabbed him by his arm.

The fake Jessica raised her hands up. "Let me explain.

You are right. I'm not Jessica."

It was Eric's turn to ask. "Then who are you?"

"I'm Giovanna. We had to swap places for her plan to work. She created a potion, and we drank it. She sent me here to get you—"

Marcus cut her off, "You drank it and you took her place. Whose place did she take?"

"Valentina's."

"Where's your mother, then?" Francesco asked.

Marcus tried to control his anger and fear as he fisted his hands and ground his teeth. "Why the hell would she do something like that?"

Giovanna tried to explain, "She was afraid that Valentina would join forces with Alaric since she is clearly in love with him," she said the last words, staring at her father. "Mom is fine. We have her locked up somewhere else, and she'll be delivered to you to do whatever you think is appropriate. But only after we're sure Alaric won't be after her any longer."

Francesco had a scowl on his face, but after Giovanna's explanation, he simply turned his back on them and walked to the opposite side of the living room where he seemed to be contemplating the wall.

Marcus looked at the fake Jessica again. "Tell me what Jessica's plan is and how we can help."

Eric intervened, "Did they take her already? Is that what you are following on your screen? Did you use a tracking device? What if it fails?"

"How far is Kevin?" Marcus asked, staring at his son.

"He's close. He's bringing air support."

"Is Jessica safe?" Marcus glared at Giovanna.

The girl nodded. "Alaric needs her to break the bond. She's safe until then."

"Are you relying solely on a tracking device that can be removed?" Marcus asked.

"If you let me explain everything before jumping to conclusions, I can debrief you about what's going on," the girl boldly stated. The king nodded, encouraging her to proceed. "I have to change back to my old self first. I can see it's bothering you, and I no longer need to pretend to be her."

"Do what you need to do?" Marcus stated, stepping aside to let her pass.

"I'm going to grab some equipment, too," the werewolf said as he walked behind Giovanna and entered a room.

Marcus turned to face his son.

Eric looked from his phone to him. "I've texted Kevin to tell him what's going on. He'll wait for directions to know where to go."

Sighing, Marcus unfolded his arms and mussed his hair. "I really hope we can find her and free her before that lunatic finds out she's Jessica."

"It was a risky and bold move," Eric said with a worried expression.

The sound of the boots on the pavement alerted them that Giovanna was returning, but before she could say anything, Francesco sped to her side and grabbed her arm.

"I need to talk to your mother right now. You need to

tell me where she is or take me there. I've been agonizing for days. The things she said—"

Giovanna cut him off, "She meant every word and you know she did. She needs to be punished. Your relationship can't continue like this. She keeps hurting us with her hate."

"I tried to reason with her on several occasions. You know I did. She doesn't want to forgive me for my actions in the past."

"It's been ages, literally."

Marcus cleared his throat. "We don't have time for this."

Giovanna removed her arm from her father's grasp. "Once I do my part and help in saving Jessica, I'll personally take you to see Mom. But, for now, we have more pressing matters to address."

The serious expression on the girl's face made her father step back and nod in agreement.

Looking at the king, Giovanna said, "Uncle, everything is happening according to plan. As long as the tracker works, we will find where they are taking Jessica."

"I would feel better if she had opened her mind link. I can't see anything," Marcus complained.

"Maybe they drugged her," the girl said. "Maybe she's unconscious."

"I'm following her signal, it's strong and steady. We'll have her location soon enough," the werewolf informed as he stepped back into the living room with a tablet in his hands and a backpack hanging on his shoulder. "I'm

Liam, by the way, one of Jessica's friends."

Marcus nodded to him, and Eric reached out to shake his hand.

Eric stared at the tablet before asking, "How is your team communicating with each other?"

"We are using earpiece communicators. I have a few more to give to you and your dad. You'll need them to coordinate the attack with Sebastien's pack."

"Kevin will need one, too. He's bringing backup from Chicago," Eric informed.

"It will take them too long to get here. We are assuming Alaric's hideout is not far from here. Based on Myra's information, we were able to track their movements, and we are pretty sure they are hidden somewhere on the outskirts of Boston."

"Kevin's boss lent us two choppers and, assuming this tracker is right, Alaric's men are heading to the coast."

"Oh, that's really helpful. We may need air support to track down the enemies if they try to escape."

Marcus interrupted their chit-chat. "My men are waiting downstairs. We need to get in the cars and follow where they're going. As soon as they stop, and we have the exact location, we can set a perimeter and instruct our combined forces on how to attack."

Liam nodded. "As soon as they stop, I'll have satellite images to work with."

"Great," Marcus said as he walked to Liam and grabbed him by his shirt and forced him to follow him. "The tech wizard is coming with me." He looked at the werewolf. "I want you to give me one of those earpieces, so I can listen to what is going on and find out who's your team leader."

"Gio-vanna is our team le-ader," Liam stuttered as he followed him outside the apartment.

## CHAPTER ELEVEN—TRAPPED

## JESSICA

Her head hurt, and she had a bad taste in her mouth when she came to her senses. Blinking, she focused her blurry eyes and realized that they had left her in a dark room with old gray walls and a wooden floor. There was only a chair and a small round table in the middle of the fifteen by fifteen sized space. They had uncovered her head, but they had left her in a sitting position, leaning against the wall with her hands still cuffed. Despite the shut blinds, there was light coming from a small lamp on the table.

She wiggled, but her head hurt because of the blow that made her unconscious, the moment she entered the vehicle.

Feeling her mouth dry and her body grow weak, she tried to focus on what she had to do. She needed to establish a mind-link with Marcus. She needed to tell him where she was or, at least, give him a beacon to follow. She hoped the tracker she had ingested was working properly and would lead her team to rescue her.

Maybe it had been a bad idea because she was terrified. Fear was seeping into her body and making her heart race. Wherever she was, she was sure that, soon enough, she was going to be face to face with Alaric. Only then, she would understand what she had to do and how she could unbind him from his soul-mate.

"Marcus…" she whispered, trying to focus her thoughts on him and ignoring the pain and the white noise. "Marcus…"

The reply was a constant buzzing sound in her ears. Her beloved wasn't answering her. Maybe she was too weak. Maybe there were protective runes preventing her from using her powers.

Looking around, she willed her feet to move and her body to stand up. She needed to know where she was and if the door was locked. She needed to touch the wooden door, concentrate, and feel her surroundings. After all, the silver cuffs were only made to drain a vampire of their force, but she wasn't a vampire. Therefore, she was able to tap into her magic and use it to help her understand how many men Alaric had there. She wasn't running. She wanted to meet the bastard face to face. She wanted him to think she was Valentina, play the dangerous game, and stall if she had to.

Noises of footsteps made her lower her head and close her eyes to pretend she was still unconscious. The door opened after a key turned inside the lock. More footsteps, heavy and impatient. Her body was moved when a male grabbed her by her arms and made her sit in the chair.

"Wake up, bitch." It was a direct command followed by a slap on her face. She shook in pain only to open her eyes and hiss at him. The guy stepped back, caught off guard, as he yelled, "Secure her to the chair."

"Calm down, Simon. She's trapped and weak,"

another man beside him informed, pointing at her hands sitting on her lap, imprisoned by the shackles.

"Where the fuck am I?" she asked, trying to sit down properly and glaring at the two vampires in front of her. They were tall and ugly, more beasts than men with scarred faces and turned up noses, thin lips, and brown eyes. They were both the same height but dressed differently. While one appeared to be some bad ass biker, the other was wearing blue jeans and a dark t-shirt.

"She's pretty. What does the master want her for?" the calmed one asked. He had one eye slightly bigger than the other, maybe it was due to a punch or a wound someone inflicted on him when he was human.

"The master would cut our balls off and feed them to us if we touched her," the rude and impatient one said. "Hector, just go tell the commander that she's awake. Maybe when master is finished with her, we can play, too." He smirked wickedly.

That Simon fellow and his twisted friend were on her top list to be disposed of. More than murderers, Jessica hated rapists. By the sly stare and snorts both were exchanging, it was common practice to them to abuse and rape women. Too bad she couldn't get rid of them just yet. She needed to make sure Alaric was there, and she could unbind him before the team arrived to finish him off.

## CHAPTER TWELVE—TRACKING

## MARCUS

The king was extremely quiet since they left the flat that Jessica and her team were using as a hideout. However, the lines on his face couldn't conceal how worried he was.

"Still nothing?" Eric asked as his eyes focused on his father's expression.

"I can't hear her. Maybe she's still unconscious."

"It's been ten minutes since they stopped. I'll have satellite images in two minutes," Liam said from the front seat where he had his laptop on his lap and was typing.

"The tracker worked. We'll know where Alaric is keeping her in a few moments," Eric said.

Marcus knew his son was trying to calm him.

"I know, son," Marcus whispered, leaning further on the car door and staring at the darkness outside the window. "I would be more reassured if I could know what she's doing and what's happening to her. I need to know she's still alive."

Eric assured, "She's alive. He needs her and has no idea that it's Jessica and not Valentina."

"I should have locked her up in the palace."

The king saw the reflection of Eric's smile through the window of the car. Marcus wasn't trying to be funny, though. His mate could be terrified for all he knew. He would gladly change places with her to shield her from the pain.

Eric brought him back to reality with his words. "She wouldn't like that. We may not like to have Mom in harm's way but her idea made it possible for us to catch Alaric and make him pay for all the wrong he did."

"Death isn't punishment enough for what he did," Marcus said as he looked at his son. "When he killed a whole village, the first time, I spared him. I regretted it deeply, and I have to live with the magnitude of my mistake. The last thing I want is to lose your mother, again, because of him. She found a way to get back to us. I should have protected her more, convinced her to stay instead of taking it upon herself to stop Alaric."

"Alaric destroyed her family because of what Valentina did to him. Wanting it or not, Jessica would go after Alaric even if she wasn't Isobel's reincarnation."

The king sighed and rubbed his forehead, closing his eyes. "What is Anna and Shane's status?"

Liam asked, "Do you want your earpiece to talk to her?"

"Not yet. I need to concentrate on hearing Jessica. I don't want any other voices preventing me from that."

"Anna, how are things going over there?" Eric asked, tapping the earpiece in his ear. He nodded to what he heard and then informed his dad, "They are parking the car and going on foot. They will report back in a few minutes."

"Tell her to be careful. Alaric might have a lot of traps

around his property and there will be men patrolling."

Eric nodded and transmitted his message. "Anna said to tell you that she loves you too."

Marcus grinned. "I just want her to be safe."

"She knows, Dad."

"Eric, as soon as we arrive, I want you coordinating with the team from the outside. You are staying in the car with Liam. I'm the only one who is going in to rescue your mom. I don't want to worry about your safety, too. No." He shook his head, raising his hand so Eric wouldn't speak. "You need to rule the town if anything bad happens to me, and you will need to take care of your mother. Promise me you'll stay behind."

"Nothing will happen to you, Dad."

"In the eventuality of something happening, my orders are clear."

Eric nodded.

\* \* \*

## ANNABEL

The clouds covered the moon and the absence of artificial illumination made the night darker and everything seem lonelier. Nevertheless, darkness wasn't a problem for a vampire or a werewolf. Anna and Shane could rely on it to be able to arrive unannounced to wherever the tracker was taking them.

The night was humid, creating a fog that made the spider webs shine whenever the moon peeked out behind a cloud. Meadows and trees were the only things that surrounded this place. They had to run through the woods, carrying their weapons in a backpack while they climbed and sniffed the air for danger. It was essential to stay away from the main roads and be on the lookout for traps and camouflaged sentinels. Adrenaline pumped through their veins and all their senses were aimed at their surroundings.

Anna climbed trees and jumped from branch to branch while warning Shane about what lay in front of them. A couple miles ahead, and they had arrived at their destination without encountering any enemy or even having to hide from a patrol.

Shane stopped at approximately thirteen feet from the wall that prevented them from moving forward. Meanwhile, Anna jumped from a tree and landed next to him in a crouched position. They were both silent with eyes frozen on the wall ahead which was almost as tall as the trees. That fortification could be the reason for the lack of security around Alaric's lair.

"Shall we climb it?" Shane proposed.

"We need to find the entrance to let the others in. We have no idea if there are surveillance cameras along the wall. We need to report and find a gate. Then, we go in and try to enter the compound without raising suspicion. It will be hard. We can't use Myra's appearance."

"Maybe we can use someone else's appearance, one of the guards outside."

Anna said, "We can try. Just wait here. I want to have an idea of what awaits us behind this wall."

"What are you going to do?" Shane asked, watching Annabel running back to the woods.

Gaining momentum, she sped ahead, and with a jump, she gripped the wall. While digging her fingers in the hard rock, she climbed her way to the top. Then, she used her arms to lift her up and crouch on top, where she looked around carefully, using her enhanced hearing to detect any camera moving around.

In the distance, she noticed the huge house made of rock on the slope of the mountain with a daunting view of the abysmal cliff. There were trees and rocks separating her from the house that looked more like a stronghold than a manor. There was also a tree-lined road which led to the mansion. Therefore, there was an entrance and probably a huge gate with guards and cameras.

Anna tried to imprint in her mind the image of the layout, so she could find the best way to get to the house. She also wanted Shane to see what she was seeing. Then, she backflipped with the elegance of a feline and landed on the ground, where Shane was waiting for her.

"We move east to the gate. We neutralize the guards and get in," Shane whispered.

Anna nodded, dusting her half-finger gloves against her leather coat.

"Then," he said, grabbing her hand and squeezing it, "you will look for Jessica, and I'll neutralize the guards in the mansion to prevent them from sounding the alarm before the others arrive here."

Anna nodded again.

"And you will promise me to be careful."

"This is not my first time invading a dangerous facility with enemies wanting to take me down," she informed him, but she lost the straight face and smiled at him because she knew he was only showing how much he loved her. "I'll be careful, honey."

"We should have brought more help."

"It's a stealth operation. Another person would ruin our synergy and would probably mess up. I have faith in you, and we can share information with our mind-link."

"I'm betting there are a lot of guards inside the perimeter. More help would come in hand. Nevertheless, we'll work with what we've got, and Eric just told me that they will be here in twenty minutes to half an hour."

"Then we have to hurry up. We don't want Alaric to run, do we?"

"No, we don't. Let's go."

## CHAPTER THIRTEEN—TWISTED


## ALARIC

Alaric woke up with a start. It had been a while since he had nightmares about his mother's death. He couldn't erase her look of terror from his mind, every time he remembered how he pushed her from a balcony because he was upset with her refusal to leave with him. Jessica's arrival had brought bad memories and opened old wounds, but he wasn't finished with her. This time, she might have eluded him because he hated Valentina more than her. Yet, the moment he didn't need Valentina anymore, he would spare no expense to find the witch and finish her off. It wouldn't be that hard, really. She was most likely going back to his father's lands.

The absurdity in all of that was still resonating in his mind. *What could my father possibly be thinking, dating the girl and wanting to replace my mother?* No one could replace his mother. The king was probably becoming senile in his old age.

Alaric rolled in bed, staring at the ceiling. It was night. He had fallen asleep while waiting for his men to bring Valentina to his house. They had strict orders, and he knew they wouldn't disobey him and mess things up. He was also calmer now that he had Beth with him.

He rolled his hand around the chain that he was holding tight even while sleeping. The chain was attached to a dog collar that was around Beth's neck. She still needed to be punished for what she had done to serve as an example to others. The collar around her neck was a way to remind her that she belonged to him and had to obey him. After the binding, she would become a lot easier to handle. She would finally accept her feelings for him, and they could be happy. The three of them would be a happy family, four if he included his unborn son.

Alaric wrapped the chain around his hand, one more time, pulling Beth against his body. She gagged. Holding on to the dog collar with both hands, she tried to breathe as she woke up.

"I don't like you so far from me. I've told you that before." His voice was hoarse.

He loosened the grip and placed an arm around her shoulders, ignoring her whimpers of pain. "You should stop being stubborn and drink blood. The girl is breathing and there is still blood to take from her," he mumbled, moving his arm to point at the unconscious and half-naked girl who was on the floor next to his bed. "I brought her as a gift to you. You would heal if you fed."

Beth said nothing.

He didn't know if he should slap her or kiss her. She had been too quiet since he brought her from the dungeons.

Sighing, he reasoned, "She's a blood slave. They are just good to feed on and fuck. Fucking her meant nothing to me. I wouldn't have needed to fuck her if you weren't acting like such a bitch and pretending that you didn't enjoy it when I touched you. You even liked it when I fucked her in front of you. She did. She moaned really well for me. You should learn to moan like her."

\* \* \*

**BETH**

"Just let me take her to the infirmary," Beth spoke, trying to conceal the disdain in her voice but failing miserably. Alaric was a conceited prick, and he often mistook grief and pain for pleasure.

"We have servants to do that. Your place is by my side, in my bed, and following me around like an obedient little bitch."

"Then let me call a servant."

"No!"

Beth didn't speak again. She tried to ignore the pain that was blazing throughout her body and crippling her. The collar was making her feel even more uncomfortable. She tried to ignore his presence in bed, the girl dying on the floor, and her miserable existence. But Alaric wasn't done talking.

"There aren't any more reasons for you to starve yourself to death. Just eat before I force you to."

"Take her to the infirmary, and I'll feed on another slave."

"Do you think you can negotiate with me?" Alaric clasped his hand around her face and made her look into his red eyes. She gulped but didn't complain. He narrowed his eyes as he let her go. Getting up from the bed, he pulled on the chain. His pull made her stumble over the bed and almost fall down onto the floor. Meanwhile, he leaned down over the girl's body, grabbed her by the head, and snapped her neck, thus killing the blood slave.

The air left Beth's lungs, and she was unable to control the anger. "You bastard, you fucking bastard! You heartless and deranged lunatic!"

Alaric smirked to her inflamed words. Anger had given her strength to rise from the bed and stand without stumbling.

His voice came out smooth, contradicting her outburst. "That's so much better. See how you still have it in you?" He kneeled on the bed, in front of Beth, grabbing her by her shoulders and forcing her to get closer. "They are just food, nothing more. Now, stop being stubborn and feed."

"No!"

"I think you need another lesson," he whispered darkly, putting his hand between her legs and cupping her sex. He moved his thumb in circles. "Don't fight it. I know how you like it. You enjoyed yourself in the bathtub when I washed you. You were filthy," he whispered in her ear, forcing his hand further up and preventing her from closing her legs. "I washed you and then I licked you really good, and you moaned. I'll make you moan again."

"Doesn't mean I liked it," she muttered between her

teeth, clenching her jaw and fisting her hands harder until her knuckles were white.

"Just admit it, you want me."

"Yes," she said, leaning closer to his ear, "impaled through your heart and bleeding to death."

Alaric growled, clearly upset, but instead of punching her or slapping her face, he made her stare at him. "You know what? Before the end of this night, I'll have you begging me to fuck you. Just like your sister does every time I'm with her. Have you heard her? Of course, you did. Do you remember? In the dungeon, when I first found you. Did you enjoy it?" He kissed her lips, biting her lower lip and pulling it back. She didn't respond to his provocation. He kept moving his hand, wanting to arouse her. "Moan for me, Beth. No one will hear us. Just let go."

Beth looked away and fought back the tears.

"I'm going to miss the time when you didn't beg me to fuck you. Now, lay down and take off your nightgown. And don't try to fight this, I'm not in the mood, and I might enjoy hurting you. We don't want that, do we?"

"Fuck you!"

"I'd rather fuck you," he teased, smirking and shoving her against the mattress.

He lay on top of her, placing her body under his.

Beth tried to push him off, but he was too strong and heavy for her weakened body. There was no point in fighting, she knew that, but there was still a part of her that believed she could escape him or he would kill her for good and end her misery.

Alaric stopped fighting her when someone knocked at his door. It was a shy knock. He raised his head and concentrated in the movement outside. "Who is it?"

"It's Conrad, sir. The witch has arrived, and she's awake."

"I guess that Vincent's replacement was able to follow my orders. We'll have to play later unless you can't wait. Are you horny, Beth?" She pushed him away, and he laughed. "Give me ten minutes, Conrad. I'm kind of busy."

Beth's face lost its color. She looked at him, heart shrinking because she wasn't going to escape as she thought.

"You need to learn that nothing is going to save you from me. You belong to me, and we are going to be together, forever. Now, stop fighting me or there won't be any baby coming out from your sister's womb, at least, not by the natural method. I'll just rip him out of her and choke it in front of you. Would you like that?"

This time, Beth cried. Tears ran down her cheeks and her chest contracted in pain.

"Now, tell me how much you love me and how much you want me."

"I love you. I want you." Her voice came out strangled.

"Moan, baby," he ordered, as he lifted the skirt of her nightgown. Before Beth could say anything else, Alaric was pulling his boxers down his legs and was taking her. "Hot and moist. So moist," he exhaled against her neck.

"Moan," he ordered, moving faster.

Beth cried more, closing her mouth to conceal the sobs. There wasn't much difference for Alaric if she was crying in pain or moaning in pleasure. For him, it was all the same. He just liked to abuse. He got aroused by it. She kept crying until he finished, put his clothes on, and left, but not before ordering her to get dressed for the ritual and telling her how happy they would be together.

## CHAPTER FOURTEEN — THE FACE TO FACE

### ALARIC

Alaric entered the small room, where his men were keeping Valentina, with his commander closer by. His old lover was looking at the floor, her hands cuffed on her lap, and her black hair falling wildly down her face. She was still a stunning woman. Being a vampire only improved her looks. They had fun together until he decided that their futures weren't as linked together as Valentina thought and wanted.

"Are you ready to undo the harm you did?" Alaric asked, making her stare at him with serene and observant eyes. She didn't look scared. There was a glint of defiance in her posture.

"I guess I don't have any other choice," she said, smirking at him.

He frowned and put his arms behind his back. Valentina narrowed her eyes as if analyzing his reactions.

Arching an eyebrow, he asked, "Do you still hate me?"

"Does it matter?"

"Aren't you afraid I might kill you?"

"Don't you think I know you will?"

"So why aren't you scared?"

"You need me, and I can help you a lot more alive than dead, even after doing the spell you want me to do."

Alaric smirked. "That's a cocky statement."

"I can help you with Jessica. I know you aren't happy with your dad marrying the witch."

Straightening up, he shrugged. "I'll think about it. I may be nicer to you if your spell of binding another soul to my own soul works."

"What do you mean?" Valentina's expression changed.

Alaric crouched down in front of her, speaking in a secretive manner. "Do you remember when you wanted us to be soul-mates?"

She nodded.

"I found someone I want more than the pathetic soul-mate the gods designed for me. I need you to set me free from the curse because I don't like to be vulnerable, but then, I want you to bind my soul to another woman."

Valentina didn't speak, she seemed to be thinking. "What will you give me in return for that?"

Alaric sneered. *The nerve of the former witch.* "Your life, maybe. But you are in no position to make demands."

Against all odds, Valentina smirked. "I thought you'd be more upset to see me."

He frowned. "Why?"

"You and I have a history together. I put a curse on you."

Alaric stood up with a grin. "I'm feeling happy today. I got something back that I wanted for a long time."

"What is that?"

"You'll meet her."

"Can you remove these shackles, then? They are

uncomfortable."

"I guess they are kind of pointless. But I don't want you feeling too comfortable."

Valentina argued, "I'll need my hands free to perform the ritual."

"Yes, you will." Alaric stared at the two men behind him. "One of you, go see if the attic where the ritual will be held is ready. And get my wife out of bed and escort her there."

"I need to see the book," Valentina said, looking sideways at the guy who left after Alaric's command. "To look for the second spell."

That got Alaric's attention. "Don't you remember it by heart?"

"I have better things to do these days than memorizing spells."

"You sound and act different," he said. Valentina didn't blink to his sudden remark. "There is something off about you."

"Funny, you are a lot more composed than I expected. Everybody told me how mad you were, not to talk about the homicidal tendencies. You still sound as crazy as you were before, though."

Alaric smirked. "You didn't think I was mad when we were sharing the same bed. In fact, you quite enjoyed my ideas to change the world."

"Not all of your ideas," Valentina corrected him.

He nodded.

She added, "You betrayed me."

Lowering his head, he declared, "That's not how I

remember what happened."

"And how do you remember?"

"I have no wish to remember things about the past. I want to focus on my future. You are here to correct your stupid and pointless revenge and to obey my orders."

"Why do you think I will?"

His body tensed with her continuous disrespect. He muttered, "You know what I can do to you. You've seen what I do to my enemies. You don't want to be my enemy, do you?"

"Darling," Valentina smirked at him, her voice seemingly calm and controlled. "I don't think you have friends. You either have scared rats working for you or people trying to kill you. I was your only friend. I wanted to rule the world with you, and you betrayed me. We are enemies."

Alaric narrowed his eyes, taking her words into consideration. "There's something off about you," he said, not quite sure about what it was. "However, there is something I'm more curious about. Who is your mate? You've been hiding for ages. I thought you had died a long time ago. It came as a surprise when I saw you act like a lunatic in the video the other witch sent me. Your clothes and your jewels are exquisite. You look serene and unafraid. Do you think that someone is going to find you and save you from me? My men went through a lot of trouble to bring you here without anyone following them. They removed the trackers from you. There are protective runes on my doors. You won't be able to contact your mate by using your mind-link. I thought of that the moment I realized you had become a vampire."

Valentina narrowed her eyes, clearly upset with what he was saying. "There's a flaw in your reasoning."

Alaric tilted his head towards her, waiting for her to tell him.

"I don't want to go back to my mate."

Alaric smirked. "Why not?"

"It's a long story. But are we going to chit-chat or will you take me to your mate, so I can remove the curse?"

"And why are you so eager to do that?"

"I want you to understand that you can trust me, and I can be valuable to you. I'm a powerful witch, and we seem to have the same agenda."

"You are no longer a witch. You may be able to do some spells and potions, but you have no real power. You are a vampire now. I have no need for another vampire."

"I have access to witches."

"I have a witch."

"I have a lot more than one. Powerful witches who can help you stay hidden."

Alaric informed her about the error in her proposal. "After this night, I won't need to hide."

She kept reasoning with him. "You can't fight everybody alone. You need allies."

"I have plenty of allies. Now, stop delaying the inevitable."

Valentina smirked.

"What's so funny?"

"You have no idea of how many people there are who

want your head, do you?"

"Other purebloods vampires are sympathetic to my cause. These new trendy ideas of acceptance are going to fade away. Our bloodline needs to be protected and hybrids need to be killed. They are an anomaly."

Valentine yawned. "Save me the speech, I know it by heart."

"Are you going to perform the ritual or do you need some persuading?" Alaric questioned.

Valentina scowled with boredom. "Let's get this over with."

Alaric was going to turn around and leave but curiosity stopped him. "There is something I would like to know before I leave."

"What?"

"Who hid you all these years? Who is your mate?"

Valentina's eyes lit up, and she smiled impishly. "It's a funny thing, actually. We are family since I married your uncle."

"Which uncle?"

"Your mother's brother, Francesco."

"So, Uncle Francesco is mated to a witch, and he's been keeping it a secret for all these years? Interesting. Have you got any offspring?"

"No."

"Don't lie to me!"

"A daughter."

"Did you have her when you were still a witch with my uncle?" Valentina nodded, and Alaric snarled in disgust. "A filthy hybrid. I guess it's a curse in my family. I was the only one lucky enough to have a pureblood vampire mate." Valentina was going to speak, but he held his hand up for her to hold her tongue. "Don't. I'm done with you. I just want you to be smart and do what I want. If you don't, I'll have to hurt you and hunt down your child, cut off her head, and feed her blood to you."

Valentina rolled her eyes and held her hands up. "Just take these off, they are pointless, and I'll need my hands to perform the ritual."

Alaric motioned for his man to free Valentina from the handcuffs.

Then, he spoke again, "Conrad, I'll get Beth. Make sure that Valentina arrives at the ritual room and all of the ingredients are there for the spell."

Conrad looked to the witch and signaled his man to grab her and take her away.

"I may take a while, but I'm sure you can handle a vampire without letting her escape or hurt Marie, can't you?"

Conrad bowed his head in a sign of respect, and Alaric strode his way out of the room.

## CHAPTER FIFTEEN—OBSESSION

### ALARIC

When Alaric entered his bedroom, there were two servants around Beth, helping her dress and fixing her hair. She looked stunning, wearing the golden mermaid silk dress he had picked out for her. The make-up had cleared the pale and dim look of her face. However, she didn't look any happier than when he had left. If anything, her body stiffened in alarm the moment she realized that he was there, watching her. Nevertheless, everything would change the moment Valentina performed the ritual to combine their souls. Then, he could remove the collar from around her neck and let her have some freedom.

"The witch is ready and waiting for us," he informed. "I was hoping that you would be happier with the nice dress I bought for you to wear."

"I'm extremely happy," she whispered, closing her eyes when one of the servants wanted to put a bit more eyeshadow on. "It's lovely. Yet, I don't understand why you want me to get dressed like this while wearing this ridiculous collar around my neck."

Alaric squinted, pondering if he should remove it or not. It was hurting her pretty, ivory skin. "It's a special night for us. I want you to look your best."

"I won't look my best if you keep treating me like an animal."

Alaric smirked. Despite everything that happened, Beth was still resilient in speaking her mind and rebelling against his actions. "You know why you're wearing that collar around your neck."

"The only thing I'm guilty of is killing Vincent because he wanted to kill my sister and her baby. I didn't try to run away. I...did everything you wanted." Beth folded her arms in front of her chest.

The servants had stopped and stared at the floor, clearly trembling with fear. No one dared to speak like that to him. Insubordination was dealt with cruel penalties.

"I'll free you after the spell."

Beth looked him in the eyes. She didn't normally do that.

"Now, be a good girl and stop pouting."

His words made Beth narrow her eyes and sneer at him. He waited for her to say something, but she just changed the subject. "Is Marie waiting for us?"

"Yes, you'll see your sister."

"Is the baby okay?"

"I guess." He shrugged, and her eyes lost their shine. The baby was important to her, he knew that. He wished she could feel the same preoccupation and love when talking about himself. "I'm sure the baby is fine."

Beth nodded, staring at the floor.

"I came here to get you."

"I could get there on my own."

"But I wanted to talk to you before the ritual," he clarified, motioning for the servants to leave.

They dipped their heads in obedience and, in a respectful manner, closed the door behind them.

Beth didn't look at him. She kept her gaze on the floor.

Narrowing his eyes, he debated on whether he should order her to come to him or go to her. He decided to go to her, grabbing her hands and noticing how she was startled from his touch. "I'm…sorry for earlier."

Beth tilted her head as if she was trying to decipher his words.

"I'm going to be a lot more patient once you are my mate."

"Yes, master," she said.

Alaric frowned as he put his hand under her chin, forcing her to stare at him. She gulped when they made eye contact.

"I've waited for this moment for a long time. I'm feeling happy and gracious. After this, we can move from this house, go sightseeing, or go watch a show. What do you think? Would you like that?"

Beth shrugged, speaking in a compliant voice, "Whatever you want, master."

"I couldn't trust you before, but after the binding spell, there won't be any reasons for you to want to escape from me. We can go on vacations. Marie needs somewhere quiet to ensure her pregnancy. You could use some sun yourself. You are too pale and skinny. I like you with a bit more meat. Didn't Vincent feed you?"

"He did. I just don't like to feed from the source."

"I ordered them to bring you a jar of blood," he said, looking around the bedroom. The jar was on a small table with a glass half full. "You should have drunk more."

"I'll drink later."

Alaric nodded then looked at the closed veils.

Beth asked, "What's the problem?"

"I can't quite put my finger on it, but there is something off with Valentina. She's not how I remembered her to be."

"It's been how long since you last saw her?"

"Almost two hundred years."

"People change."

"Yes, but she's too calm for someone who hates my guts."

Beth looked away before asking him, "Are you going to kill her when she finishes doing what you want?"

He put his hands in his pockets and shrugged. "I don't know. She can be useful, and she's family."

"What do you mean?"

"She's married to my uncle. Can you believe that? She's my Uncle Francesco's soul-mate. Talk about being in a small world."

Beth didn't say a thing about that. Instead, she changed the subject. "Are you really going to let the baby live?"

"Yes, Beth. If you are a good girl, I'll let your sister keep the baby. Marie will be happy to have you back by her side."

"She hates me."

"No, honey," he said, softened by her sad tone when saying those words about her sister. "We will love each other from now on. She will love you, too. We'll be a happy family.

## CHAPTER SIXTEEN—INFILTRATION

### ANNABEL

There was a single guard at the gate, and he was reading a magazine. Anna scrutinized the surroundings, looking for the hiding assault team which could be concealed to get them. Something was off, it was too easy. Shane was in her thoughts, exchanging ideas with her, assuming that Alaric was cocky enough about his safety that he didn't need many guards at the entry. Then, they talked about how they were going to neutralize the guard without sounding the alarm.

Anna wanted to feign an injury or that her car broke and she needed help, so the guard would come out, and she could knock him out cold. Shane was against the idea, noticing that it was cliché and overused in the movies. It would raise a red flag, and the guy may have orders to kill on sight. He wasn't going to put Anna's life in danger. Instead, he threw a rock, hoping the guy was curious enough to go see what was making noise. Anna face-palmed herself because of the lack of creativity, and mentally rolled her eyes, making Shane smirk.

His plan didn't work. The guy was so concentrated on reading that he didn't hear the sound of the rock falling in the bushes.

Anna focused her vision on what the guy was doing. It turned out that he was drooling over sexy and almost naked guys' pictures and not actually reading.

*"Don't even think about it,"* Shane muttered in her head, displeased with her new idea. *"Besides, he will know that I'm a werewolf and it will be suspicious all by itself."*

"Well, at least, you were right. It wouldn't work if I was the one showing up. He wouldn't fall for my charm."

*"Maybe, but I'm not going to take my shirt off just to test your theory,"* Shane replied.

Anna mentally chuckled and grabbed a bigger rock, throwing it against the gate, and startling the guy out of his chair.

The guard looked around, frantically scanning for the origin of the loud sound. Putting down the magazine, he got up and leaned against the glassed window of the gatehouse to check the night.

Another rock flew and landed in the bushes, making him jump back. He was a frightened security guard, and Anna sighed out of frustration. He would probably call someone instead of checking what was outside. She saw him reach for the phone, then retreat and put the phone down. After a moment, he grabbed a shotgun and got out. Before he could step any further, Shane appeared behind him and snapped his neck. The guard was out cold. Then, Shane pulled the body inside the gatehouse while Anna landed behind the gate, signaling him to open it so the others could get in once they arrived.

Shane opened the gate, and Anna got in. Meanwhile, he secured the guy to the chair, putting his hands behind his back with silver cuffs.

"One of us should stay behind, but I'm not going to

let you go in alone. Therefore, let's just hope that no one notices the gate is opened," Shane said as he grabbed the guy's access card and cell phone. "I think they use this to enter the house," he said, showing her the access card. "If so, it will be easier to get in."

"We still need to pass by the men patrolling the area. I'm sure there's a lot of them. See if he has a walkie-talkie somewhere."

"It doesn't look like it."

"They must communicate somehow, maybe by phone."

"He uses a code to unlock his phone."

Anna placed her backpack over a small table, opening it and taking her swords out. "You will use his appearance to go into the house. I'm going to gear up and follow the path to the main building. Meanwhile, you use the card to open the door. There must be a backdoor entrance, somewhere."

"I should go first and then tell you if it's safe or not. Count the guards…"

"No. They may find it odd that this guy is leaving his post unattended. I'll go in first and disable the guards outside. I have plenty of darts to throw around and knock them out cold."

Shane grabbed her hand. "I'm not happy with leaving you alone."

"I'm not happy either, but we don't have any other choice now that we can't use Myra and her boyfriend's appearance."

Shane stood still, his eyes showing that he wasn't

pleased with the plan.

"There will likely be other guards around the perimeter of the house. I need to take care of them," she reasoned with him.

"I could deal with them."

"You will because there will be guards along the tree path, too. We will meet at the back of the house, near the entrance."

"Fine," Shane agreed.

Smiling, she walked to the guy strapped to the chair. "Good. We need to hurry. We are losing time," she reminded him while relieving the vampire of his shirt. "Get dressed, drink the potion, and let's hurry up." Anna pierced the vampire's neck with a dart. "Just to keep us safe. This serum will knock him out when his heart restarts. It guarantees ten hours of blissful sleep… He may sound the alarm, and I don't want Alaric to run away and take Jessica with him."

Shane nodded and took off his shirt, so he could put on the guy's shirt and make the potion work with the remains of the vampire's DNA.

Walking to the desk, Anna took the rest of her gear from the bag, putting daggers behind her back, hiding small bombs inside her pockets, and placing hidden blades strapped to her left wrist. Then, she held her sword with a lanyard around her wrist which kept it from falling far from her if there was someone able to take it from her hand. However, in cases like that, she liked to put the sword knot and use it to throw her sword forward and then pull it back.

Her concentration was broken when Shane put his hands on her shoulders and turned her to face him.

"What?"

Shane spoke softly, "Things are going to get real the moment we leave this gatehouse. So, it's the last time I have the opportunity to kiss you before drinking the potion and we have to split up."

Anna nodded, placing her head against his chest as her arms surrounded him in a hug. "Try not to get yourself killed. It would suck to live without you."

"I love you, too," he whispered, leaning down and kissing the top of her head.

"I refuse to turn this into a sappy goodbye. I'm not going to die and neither are you. We are saving Jessica and then we can go back home to our boring and amazing lives."

"Okay, baby," he said, hugging her tight. She looked up to meet his face and his lips fell on hers. They kissed for a moment, hoping it wouldn't be their last moment together. "Now, tell me you love me."

"I love you," she whispered, smiling and pulling him in for another kiss.

## CHAPTER SEVENTEEN—THE RITUAL

## JESSICA

Alaric's men had taken her to a big space with rocky, dark walls and crappy illumination. There was an awful smell coming from the rotting flowers and unknown substances inside of jars with body parts and bugs. Despite the unwelcoming and nasty place, she was in, she couldn't complain that Alaric hadn't given her everything she needed to cook the potion and perform the ritual to break the curse.

Jessica was taking her time, mixing the herbs and double-checking the spell in the book, so Anna and Shane had time to arrive and save her from this mess. She wasn't expecting such a setback to her plan. Another variable looked at her from across the room with murderous eyes and obviously round belly. Alaric's mate was pregnant and the resolution of severing their bond and ending the curse was stronger since she didn't want the baby's death on her conscience. The only person missing was Alaric himself. He had left to get someone. Yet, fifteen minutes later he was still absent. She needed him present to start the ritual.

Jessica looked around, noticing four heavily armed men following her every move. Alaric's mate was seated in a chair, arms and legs restrained. It was an awkward way of treating one's mate, but maybe she wasn't that keen on being free from the curse. Maybe Alaric was just ludicrous.

"I'm here to help you. I don't know why you seem so annoyed about it," Jessica said to the girl when she was drawing symbols inside the five points of the pentagram.

"He's ready to kill me as soon as he's free from the curse," the girl muttered.

The witch stopped what she was doing and looked at her. "And the baby?" Her voice came out shaky and breathless.

"He doesn't want the baby. The only thing he wants is Beth, my bitch of a sister."

"I don't understand."

"You and I are as good as dead the moment you finish this ritual."

"Well, there's nothing I can do about it. I'm just a prisoner."

Jessica kept drawing symbols and reciting the incantations. Her hope was that Shane and Anna were able to infiltrate the premises to rescue her. She was nervous and frustrated because her mate-link was still not functioning, and she couldn't contact Marcus. However, she wasn't going to complain about her plan. She was going to suck it up and follow it until the end. It was as clear as ever that Alaric needed to be stopped, but, first and foremost, she had to break the curse and save his soul-mate and the little baby that was growing inside her belly. It was an innocent child, Marcus' and Isobel's grandchild.

* * *

Jessica watched when Alaric walked into the room
with a brunette who had a gloomy expression. She was
as beautiful as she was sad. There was a dog collar
around her bruised neck and, despite the make-up, her
face was pale and her eyes tired. She had been curious
when he told her that he wanted her to bind his soul to
someone other than his mate. But the girl didn't seem as
happy to be there as Alaric was. On the other hand,
Marie began to snarl like a wild animal when she saw
Alaric arriving with the competition. Jessica couldn't
blame his real mate. He was fooling around with
someone else while his mate was pregnant and
vulnerable. To make things worse, Marie claimed that the
other woman was her own sister.

Alaric smiled at the girl, caressing her face, and
speaking in her ear. He seemed happy, inappropriately
happy for a psychopath. The girl simply nodded,
perpetual sadness tainting her pretty face. Then, her eyes
eagerly looked around, just staring at Valentina for a bit,
without real interest, and lingering on Marie's face. The
other vampire looked away in disdain.

Jessica had no idea what Alaric thought was going to
happen by binding his soul to another vampire—not that
Jessica was willing to perform such a cruel and irrational
ritual. No wonder he had restrained his mate to the chair.
She probably wanted to kill her sister.

Jessica was beginning to feel sick to her stomach.
There was a tangible madness surrounding this place,

and Alaric's composed behavior was freaking her out.

She shuddered when his voice broke the silence. "I hope you aren't planning to trick me. I have read that spell a thousand times. I know it word for word. If you even think about changing something about it, you'll be sorry."

"There's a key ingredient missing here," Jessica said, ignoring his threats.

"Beth, wait there," he ordered, signaling to the empty part of the room.

She obeyed, eyes on the ground, and hands holding the skirt of the golden dress. Jessica felt sorry for her.

"Conrad, get Marie's blood. I'll give you mine, witch," Alaric said, stepping inside the pentagram and putting his hand over the boiling cauldron.

Jessica instructed him, "The blood must be acquired with the ritual knife. I've already consecrated it. And both types of blood need to be put inside this silver chalice."

Alaric motioned Conrad to move, but Jessica stopped him. "I have to draw the blood myself. First yours then your mate's. I thought you knew the spell by heart."

"I know the verbal spell. I have no idea about what rituals must be performed before."

"Then stop giving orders and let me do my job," Jessica said with a serious face and stern voice.

Alaric clenched his jaw, his eyes flickering between red and green. "Fine, just do whatever you want."

"Then get the hell out of my pentagram," she said, pointing her finger to the chair next to Marie.

Alaric narrowed his red eyes, growled but obeyed. He strode to the chair and sat down with squared shoulders and hands on his knees.

"Now that we have our places figured out, it's time to start the ritual. I've consecrated this *athame*," she said, showing them the silver knife. "It's not mine, but it shall do for this. I've also written the sacred symbols in the pentagram and started the potion in the cauldron. And might I say, it's extremely cliché. A simple metal pot would have done."

Jessica shut up, noticing how Alaric was becoming irritated, probably finding her babbling strange. She was getting out of character. She needed to concentrate and act like a selfish bitch with a god complex, no jokes, and no witty comebacks. She sighed, tuning her thought to reach her mate, knowing that it would be pointless, but she would feel a lot better if she had Marcus' voice in her head.

"What's the holdup?" Alaric asked, interrupting her thoughts.

"I'm channeling the energy of the goddess. Can you just shut up?" Jessica glared at him. Marie smirked and Conrad dipped his head lower to conceal his own smirk. There was a lot of love for the leader in that room.

"Do you have some death wish?" Alaric asked, clearly annoyed with the way she was talking to him.

Jessica rolled her eyes and grabbed the athame and the chalice from a small table inside the pentagram and next to the cauldron. Then, she recited words in Latin. Her hands glowed red and a mystical fog rose from inside the cauldron.

After reciting the first part of the ritual, Jessica walked to Alaric. He showed her his wrist, which she cut without any ceremony, watching the blood drop into the chalice. Then, she drew blood from Marie, who hissed and swore profanities.

"You shouldn't be upset, it's not good for the baby," Jessica whispered, putting two fingers over Marie's forehead. "Calm down," she ordered, making her fingers glow. Marie's eyes glazed over, putting a stop to the girl's bad mood. The witch looked at Alaric. "How many months along is she?"

"I have no idea," Alaric answered with a shrug.

"She's almost three months," a timid voice answered. Jessica lifted her head to see that the vampire in the golden dress had answered. "Is it safe to perform the ritual while she's pregnant?"

"I guess...but why would you care?"

"She's my sister," Beth mumbled.

"Well, I don't think she cares as much for you as you do for her."

"Stop stalling and perform the ritual. We still have a lot to do before dawn," Alaric commanded, losing his patience.

Jessica didn't say anything else. She simply strolled her way to the center of the pentagram, carrying the blood. There, she whispered incantations and mixed herbs with it while using the athame to stir the blood.

Magical words poured out of her mouth as she recited the incantation needed to break the spell.

However, nothing happened. Jessica recited again, and the Earth didn't move, there was no bang or movement of the candle lights, nothing.

"Something is wrong with this spell," she informed, pacing to check the book of spells. She read it out loud and browsed the other pages back and forward.

Alaric was tapping his fingers on the armchair, Marie was smirking like a mad girl, and Beth was nibbling her lower lip and bunching her skirt with her hands.

"What's wrong?" Alaric finally asked, making Jessica straightening up and spin around to face him.

"There's something missing from the spell. Are you sure this is the original version?"

"How the hell should I know? You were the one who wrote it! Don't you know what's missing?"

"I may be a vampire, but I don't have a photographic memory!"

Alaric got up from his chair. "I swear to you that if you are stalling, I'm going to rip your heart out and feed it to the dogs."

"You need me to break your curse."

"I still have your descendant as a backup."

"I'm the one who created this curse. I'm the one who will remove it. Just let me concentrate and stop pressuring me with your death threats and tantrums."

Alaric's eyes grew bigger as he balled his hands into fists at his sides.

"You want this to work tonight, don't you?" It was Beth speaking, shattering the uncomfortable silence with her voice. "Let the witch read the spell and concentrate.

Maybe she missed something or maybe the ritual doesn't work because she's nervous."

"Stay out of this, bitch!" Marie snarled, turning her head to face her sister. "Just kill the witch. She's tricking you."

"Shut up," Alaric ordered his mate

"If you kill her, we can't be bonded," Beth reminded him.

"One last chance, witch," Alaric declared, sitting back on the chair.

Jessica replayed the spell in her head, checked the recitation, and reminded herself of each herb and product she had put inside the cauldron. *Maybe Valentina had left something out on purpose.* It was a blood spell— something was binding it to survive along all those centuries. There must be some sort of secret ingredient or anchor. The spell required the blood of everybody involved.

"It's missing my own blood," Jessica said, grabbing the athame and cutting herself on her palm. "It should work now," she declared, putting down the dagger and wrapping tissue around her hand to stop the bleeding.

She noticed Alaric frowning at her actions. She patched the wound harder, aware that her blood kept staining the tissue. His own wound had already healed. Marie was still bleeding, since she was pregnant and her body was becoming more human and less immortal. But Valentina was a vampire, so her wound should have healed. Before Alaric could think more about it, Jessica stirred the chalice with the athame while she recited the incantation.

This time, the candles' lights flickered, making the shadows dance against the walls as the air seemed heavy. Gravity pulled her body down, pressuring and burning her skin.

"What is going on?" Marie screamed at the top of her lungs because the wind was swirling around them, tousling their hair.

Jessica kept reciting the incantation, putting all power and will into them, forcing the connection to break between them, wishing to save that baby's life by saving Alaric's mate.

"Alaric, make her stop! It hurts, my skin burns, the blood is boiling in my veins!"

Alaric had his eyes closed as he yelled, "Are you freeing us or killing us, witch?"

He tried to get up, but the witch knew he was stuck to his chair because of the pressure inside the room.

Jessica ignored his orders because she was feeling the thread that connected Alaric and Marie's two souls and was forcing it to split. Yet, despite her attempts to pull and stretch, it wasn't breaking. She summoned all of her powers, all of her magical abilities, and focused them on that thread as she opened her arms wide. The wind curled up her body as the light of the candles shimmered and danced to the sound of her words, but the thread seemed unbreakable.

# CHAPTER EIGHTEEN — INVASION

## ANNABEL

Anna had been extra careful while running through the gardens, hiding behind trees and taking out the guards who were patrolling. One by one, they fell on the floor, unconscious. Shane wasn't far, communicating through their mind-link and giving her information about the location of the remaining guards. He was also using the fake-guard's appearance to get near the guards and taking them out before they had time to ask him why he was away from his post.

Several minutes later, Anna and Shane met at the back of the house, in front of the security door that gave them access to Alaric's lair. Where there were most likely a lot more guards to eliminate.

"Eric and my men are passing the gates," Shane warned Anna.

"Good. Tell them not to make too much noise and to leave the air support on hold for now. We don't want the choppers alerting them to our presence before I have a location on Jessica."

"The king is telling us to get in. He'll join us shortly," Shane said, pressing the security card to the display.

A robotic voice ordered them, "Please state your name and place your palm over the screen."

"I have no idea what's the guy's name," Shane

whispered with widened eyes.

"Bob Simmons," Anna said, pointing at the security tag with the photo of the guy.

"Right!" he breathed out, placing his hand over the screen. "I hope this works. Bob Simmons."

"Access granted."

The door unlocked, and Anna grabbed the knob.

"Wait." Shane grabbed her by her arm and stopped her from entering. "I'll go first. We don't know how many are inside. It could be a trap or possibly be a room to store weapons."

"Okay," Anna agreed.

Shane entered and looked around.

"Look for security cameras."

"All clear," he said, motioning her to get inside.

Anna entered a long corridor with dimmed lights that seemed to end with another door.

Her mate said, "I'm changing back to my old self."

Anna nodded as Shane drank a small vial and his body morphed back to his true form. "We don't have a layout of the house, so we will need to split up to cover more ground."

"It's pointless now. They are parking in front of the house," Shane warned, listening for updates in his mind-link with his pack. "They will know we are here."

"Screw caution then. Once the alarm sounds, we don't have much time to find Jessica," Anna said, speeding inside and reaching the door on the other end of the corridor. She didn't mull over what she had to do, she just did it. She opened the door, grabbed her swords, and entered a hall with stone stairs going up and down. She decided to go up and, as soon as she climbed the stairs, she was faced with a vampire.

"Who the hell are you?" the guy asked.

Before he could react to the swords in her hands, she punched him in the stomach and turned him around, placing the blade to his throat.

Anna whispered in his ear as she pressed the blade harder against his throat, so he knew she meant business. "Hi! I'm glad I found you. I need a guide to tell me where I should go. You don't happen to have a plan of the house with you, do you?"

He asked with trembling voice, "How did you get in here?"

"I'll ask the questions."

"What do you want me to do?" Shane asked, from the bottom of the stairs. "Do you want me to go down?"

"No, we need to secure the rest of the division above. We are going upstairs. The others can deal with the other levels." Adrew blood from the vampire's neck, asking, "Where are the other guards?"

"Upstairs in the lounge and outside securing the perimeter."

"How many are there inside?"

"Twenty or thirty, I'm not sure."

"Where's Jessica?"

"Who?"

Anna rephrased her question. "Where's the witch your master brought here earlier tonight?"

"In the attic, upstairs," he said.

"Thank you," Anna said, using her free hand to stick a dart in his neck and put him out cold.

Before she sped up, Shane said, "We can't go upstairs alone. The rest of the guards are there."

"Do you want to wait for backup? Jessica can be killed when they find out we are here. We know she's in the attic. So, we need to move up," Anna said as she dragged the unconscious vampire down the stairs and placed him against a wall.

"I guess if we are careful enough, we can deal with them. Let me go first," Shane requested, holding her arm.

A voice behind them asked, "Where's Jessica?"

Shane and Anna looked back, staring at Marcus who had sped his way there and left a trail of wind behind him.

\* \* \*

## MARCUS

"Upstairs in the attic, apparently," Anna answered. "Where's Eric?"

"In the car. There were other guards outside, my men are handling it. They have entered through the front door of the house and are clearing the rooms out as we speak. We need to find Jessica."

Anna asked him, "Does your mind-link work now? Is she awake?"

"I don't know." Marcus closed his eyes and reached for his beloved. *"Jessie, honey, can you hear me? Jessie, are you here, baby? Answer me."*

"Marcus..."

It was a feeble whisper in the back of his mind, but his body tensed and his eyes opened. "She's alive. Tired but alive. I...can sense her inside the house."

"Let's move upstairs. Shane cover our back," Anna requested, throwing him her other sword. "Have you got a weapon, grandpa?"

"Yes, my claws," he said, with a serious face, his eyes turning purple and his fangs extended. "Eliminate anything or anyone who comes our way."

Anna nodded and ran next to him with Shane not far behind. Marcus' men were entering the compound, armed, and with orders to clear the perimeter and secure everybody in there. They could use lethal force if necessary.

Soon enough, the sound of shooting and fighting was heard and an alarm sounded and filled the house, alerting everybody about the invasion.

"There goes the element of surprise," Anna mumbled.

Kicking a vampire who had attacked her, she pierced her sword in his abdomen. Shane reached out and cut his head off. Three more enemies ran their way, coming from inside closed doors. Guns were shot, leaving bullet holes behind on the wall. A shotgun was fired, and Marcus lunged forward, taking down the three vampires at the same time as he relieved them of their weapons and hearts.

Speeding forward, Marcus slammed a guy against a door. The door fell from the force, and he saw two half naked human girls, crying while hugging each other. He didn't have time to be a gentleman and tell them they needn't fear him.

He turned to look elsewhere. There were plenty more doors to check and a lot more enemies there to question. Slamming an arm through a wooden door, he grabbed a vampire by his neck. He destroyed the rest of the door, stepping into the room as he looked the guy in the eyes. The vampire fought for air and gestured with his hands. Marcus realized he was holding him too hard, and the guy couldn't breathe or speak.

After getting nothing useful from the vampire, he entered the corridor and witnessed his granddaughter and Shane fighting the men who were leaving their rooms, partially dressed and half awake. The invasion had interrupted their sleep. They didn't seem aware of what was happening.

"We got this, move to the next floor," Sebastien said, appearing with his men. Their eyes were glowing menacingly, and his hands were morphed into claws to help them fight the vampires.

"Upstairs. I smell her upstairs," Sebastien informed with a guttural voice as the animal in him took over of his facial features.

Marcus didn't have to hear Sebastien twice. He was already climbing the stairs, paying attention to the sounds around him. He eluded the bullets that came from above, narrowing his eyes and launching himself against the vampire holding the gun. He ripped his throat, splattering blood around him and tainting his coat. He used the vampire's body as a shield against the round of bullets coming from someone else with a gun. A dart buzzed near his ear, flying across the corridor and hitting the shooter in his forehead. The guy's eyes rolled around, his mouth dropped open as he fell back.

The king tossed his improvised shield aside and nodded in appreciation to his granddaughter. They continued on.

"Too many doors," Anna sighed, staring at the corridor. "There's no more stairs. The attic must be here."

"It doesn't look like an attic to me," Marcus said, looking around.

"Maybe there's a secret door or there are stairs to the attic in some other division of this floor."

"I'm not liking this," Marcus declared as he grabbed one of Anna's daggers that were stuck in her belt and threw it across the corridor, hitting a new vampire in his forehead.

"Nice aim," Anna said, patting his shoulder.

"They are like rats, hidden everywhere. We need to be careful."

"Smoke grenades," Shane said, climbing the stairs and joining them with six grenades in his hands. "Open the door and toss it inside. It will blind them."

"Two for each of us," Anna said, grabbing her pair.

"I'm going to start at the back," Marcus warned, grabbing his grenades and speeding to the end of the corridor.

One by one, the doors were opened and the grenades tossed inside. They waited against the wall, protecting themselves from possible gunshots coming from the other side of the doors. Some of the sectors had enemies who came out coughing, but there were no signs of Jessica or Alaric.

Opening the door to an empty room, Shane said, "She's been here. I can smell her really well."

Marcus sped to him and checked the small room with a chair and a table for furniture. "Can you catch her scent and tell us where they took her?"

"There are too many vampires in this place. My senses are all over the place."

Marcus pressed on his earpiece. "Eric, secure the perimeter around the house, extend tracking teams to the gardens and make sure there are no secret passages where they can get away from the house. Understood?"

"Yes, Dad," Eric replied on the other side.

Marcus directed his attention to Shane and Anna. "Where is the library of this place or Alaric's bedroom, does anyone know?"

"The bedrooms were downstairs," Shane said, shrugging.

Marcus gruffed, "Do you have satellite images, Liam?"

"Yes," the boy responded from the other side of his communicator.

Marcus pressed his earpiece harder. "Are they in real time, can you track the enemies' movements?"

"I can detect heat signatures inside the house."

Before Marcus could say anything else, the house shook and everybody had to keep their balance.

Anna said as she held her back against the wall. "Jessie is here, somewhere."

"That's magic at work. She's in trouble or she's performing some sort of ritual," Marcus said more to himself than anything else. He squinted. "Liam," he barked. "Check the top floor for heat signatures."

"*Marcus, Marcus.*" Jessica invaded Marcus' thoughts.

"*Jessie, where are you?*"

"*Upstairs...*"

"*We are upstairs.*"

"*Look behind the fireplace. Hurry, I can't hold it much longer.*"

Her voice sounded tired. The link broke and Marcus ordered, "Fireplace. Find a fireplace. Shane, go downstairs and tell the others to look for a fireplace."

"It's an old house, there must be hundreds of them," Anna said.

Shane had already run down the stairs to warn the others, and Marcus was speeding his way down the corridor to look for a fireplace.

"Both the library and the bedroom have fireplaces," Anna shouted from across the corridor.

"The library is the most common and probable option," the king said, rushing to her side. Behind the door, he found a sumptuous library. "I see his tastes haven't changed. He still likes expensive stuff."

"Are we going to break the fireplace down?" Anna asked.

The house shook again but not as strong as the first time.

Marcus said, worried, "She's getting tired. Whatever she's doing, it's draining her. I can feel it. We need to hurry up. Once she's vulnerable, Alaric won't hesitate to kill her."

"There's a lot of heat signatures upstairs from where you are," Liam said in the com.

"There must be an attic," Anna assumed.

Feeling distressed, the king punched the wall next to the fireplace.

Anna tried to find a way to open the secret passage that gave access to the attic. "I've tried everything, candelabras, statues, and even the books on the shelf of the fireplace."

Marcus growled impatiently, pressing his hands against the tiles on the fireplace, looking for an opening switch.

"It can't be that obvious," his granddaughter said as she looked at the medieval full suit of armor holding a sword next to the fireplace.

She didn't waste any time and moved its arms, looking for the switch. Whatever Anna did, a dry sound was heard and the wall behind the fireplace began to move, opening into a dark hall with stairs.

Marcus sped up the stairs, rushing to save Jessica, at any cost.

# CHAPTER NINETEEN—RESCUE TEAM

## JESSICA

Jessica kept forcing the thread that connected Alaric and Marie's souls to break. She ignored the background noise of the girl screaming. It couldn't hurt that bad since she was the one experiencing the consequences of trying to break a black magic spell. Alaric's mate was being disruptive and trying to prevent her from separating them. It was only natural since she knew that he was planning to kill her after. Not that Jessica would let him do that. Not that she would let him bind his soul with some other innocent woman, either. But she wanted to break the connection so her friends and her own soulmate could rid the world of Alaric's malefic presence.

Suddenly, amid the veil of pain and magical power, she felt Marcus in her mind. He reached out to her and filled her thoughts with his concerned voice.

"Marcus." His name left her lips, making her skin ripple with love and sadness for being apart from him.

The alarm rang as Jessica opened her eyes and saw Alaric trying to get up from his chair. Alaric's men were also fighting against the heavy gravity that restrained them against the wall.

The cavalry had arrived before she was able to sever the bond.

"I'm going to kill you, witch, whoever you are!"

Alaric's words didn't scare Jessica as much as he wanted them to. For the moment, he was at her mercy, and she was at her full strength. Even if she drained all of her magical power, she had to keep him there until backup arrived. Draining her powers would leave her vulnerable, but she needed to save the life of that baby, before someone plunged a sword through Alaric's heart, also killing Marie and the child.

Jessica yelled at him, "Your mate isn't letting me break the curse! I'm trying to separate your soul from hers with all my strength."

Magical light surrounded Jessica's body as the rest of the attic was swept by a powerful wind.

"Marie, stop fighting," he shouted at her, unable to get free from Jessica's hold.

"She's a fake. She led them to you. Kill her!" the crazy pregnant vampire yelled. "She's not here to help us. She's here to kill us."

Her words had some effect on him because he yelled, "Conrad, stop the witch."

Jessica's eyes aimed at Conrad. He was grabbing Marie's chair, trying to enter the consecrated pentagram to obey his master. Moving one of her hands, she swirled it and sent a wave of invisible power that sent Alaric's minion slamming against the wall. It didn't knock him out, but he seemed disoriented.

Alaric recoiled in his seat as Jessica twisted her hand again. The two vampires guarding the top of the stairs fell on the floor with broken necks.

Jessica's eyes focused on Beth. The woman looked

surprised, but she didn't move to do anything that could be suspicious.

"Are you really here to kill me, Mother?" Jessica's attention was on Alaric who had professed those words. "You aren't Valentina. She's no longer a pure witch, she can't use her powers, and your hand is still bleeding from the cut. You must be Jessica."

"I don't possess the full extent of your mother's memories to be moved by your words," Jessica warned him. "All I want is to have my revenge for what you did to my family and your own family. I can't love a son who killed me in another life and killed his baby sister."

Alaric screamed at her with red eyes, "You said you had no memories. How can you remember that?"

"I remember it from nightmares and dreams I have from my past life. You may not believe that I was your mother but, trust me, I'm not keen on remembering that you were my son either. Even if I remembered everything, it doesn't change the fact that you are a psychopath, and you need to die."

"Then kill me," he dared her, smirking as if she was no threat to him. "You were always weak. You are trying to save a child I don't want, and a woman I despise."

"And who do you love? Her?" Jessica asked, pointing her hand at Beth. The vampire girl fell on her knees, screaming in pain.

Alaric lost his smile as he said, "Nothing you can do to her will be worse than whatever I already did to her."

Jessica lessened her grip on the girl, shocked by his words.

Alaric added in rage, "However, if you kill her, I won't just kill you, I'll skin you alive!"

"You really are a monster," Jessica stated, caught inside his red eyes and flustered face. The outburst and menace surprised her, though. He cared for Beth.

"We'll catch up some other day. Now, it appears I have unwelcomed visitors in my home," Alaric declared, moving his arm to reach a panel in the right arm of his seat. He flipped the panel open and pressed down on a circular button. The floor shook beneath their feet, secret passages on the wall opened to let other vampires in, and the platform beneath Alaric and Marie's chairs began to descend.

"Marie," Beth screamed in panic as she rushed to her sister's side.

"Bring Beth with you," Alaric screamed to his men, who were trying to understand what they had to do. "Stop the witch and anyone who tries to enter this room."

Jessica counted the vampires who had joined them. She also noticed that the platform wasn't descending fast enough. If she disposed of her enemies, she could reach it in time. Yet, before she could move, she heard the sound of the Mad Hatter laughter that came from Alaric when he pressed a new button and something behind her exploded and threw her forward.

The blast only made her dizzy. But it was enough to throw her to the ground, in a vulnerable position. Holding her head, she pressed her free hand against the floor and sent a wave of kinetic energy that spread across the lines of the pentagram and threw back the vampires, preventing them from reaching her. She closed her eyes and concentrated, imagining a power field surrounding her. Blood dripped from her nose as the vampires slammed their bodies against the invisible protection. Her mind focused on her mate. She needed help. Strength was abandoning her as she heard the humming of the vampires speeding around her too fast. The sound of scratching rock reached her ears, and Marcus' voice echoed inside her mind.

Opening her eyes, she saw ashes falling around her protection and caught the blur of other familiar figures who had arrived to save her. Relief washed over her as she lowered her shield and lay on the floor, exhausted.

"Where is he?" Anna asked as she looked around. "And why is there a hole in here?"

"He had some sort of elevator to take him down," Jessica explained, coughing and raising her head to look for Marcus.

The air shifted behind her back, when she tilted back her head, a vampire flew through the air and hit the wall. Marcus appeared beside her and helped her up.

"Marcus…" Jessica's eyes welled with tears. Before she could cry and tell him how much she had missed him, he was securing her against his chest.

"You are alive." He caressed her hair as he tightened the embrace. "I was worried sick."

"We can't lower our guard," Anna said. "We don't know how many other vampires will show up from the two secret doors in the brick wall."

"We need to stop Alaric. He went down the hole," Jessica said, holding her hands on his chest and pushing back so she could breathe and talk. "He just left. We need to go after him," she told Marcus as he circled her waist and prevented her from falling. She was dizzy and the room seemed to be moving under her feet.

"Calm down. You are exhausted and in pain. I can feel it."

"Where's the other vampire woman?" Jessica asked, regaining her composure and looking around. "She must know where they are going."

Marcus asked with a worried expression as he tried to prevent her from moving, "What other vampire woman?"

"Did you kill her?"

"No. I didn't kill any woman."

"Her name is Beth. She was just here. Alaric's minions must have taken her."

"Beth?" Anna's head turned to Jessica, and she walked to her side. "Dulce said something about Myra asking us to save Beth. But, she said she would be in the dungeons. Sebastien was going downstairs to look for her."

Jessica's attention was on her friend. "She was here with us. Why does Myra want to save the vampire?"

"She said Beth saved her, and that she knew about our plan. She saved Myra's life and killed Vincent. Without her help, your plan would be discovered and Myra's cover would have been blown," Anna explained.

"What the hell! I just hurt her!" Jessica shook her head

and tried to focus. She still felt dizzy, but Marcus' hands on her waist helped her stand. "Follow the other passageways and..." Before she could finish talking, Anna was already jumping into the platform where the empty chairs were.

"There's a reinforced door behind a shelf. It must lead to more stairs which must lead to gateway tunnels," Anna yelled, so they knew what she was seeing in that other room. "They closed the door behind them. We'll need to open it to go after them."

"Help me get downstairs," Jessica asked Marcus.

"You are hurt and bleeding."

"Where?" she asked, putting her hand on her forehead and noticing that there was blood there. Her hand trembled when her eyes shut down momentarily. "I'm feeling lightheaded."

"We heard an explosion. There is debris not far from us. The blast might have caused you internal bleeding, and you might have a concussion."

"I'll see a doctor when this is over. Now, we can't let him escape. But, we can't kill him either."

"He's not going to get away alive from this house, no matter what you've remembered about him, honey," Marcus said with a stern voice even if his eyes showed compassion and love for her.

"You're not understanding. His mate is pregnant. If we kill him, we will kill our grandson."

"I'm going to follow him downstairs," Anna said, still in the lower secret floor.

"Not alone, you will not," Shane protested, appearing

from one of the secret passages on the wall. "This only goes downstairs to another bedroom. But the vampire who escaped using this door was already killed downstairs. Sebastien's men caught him."

"Was Beth with him?" Jessica asked.

"There was no female with him. He was alone," Shane informed.

"Are you going to take too long coming down?" Anna questioned.

"I'm coming, baby," Shane said, jumping on the platform.

"We are going, too," Jessica said, moving forward and being held by Marcus against his chest. "They will need me to immobilize him and make sure he won't hurt anyone. I still need to finish the spell to end his curse. We need to grab Alaric and then I need to have a conversation with Valentina. The bitch is toying with us. The spell didn't work."

"You need to calm down," Marcus whispered, hugging her and placing his chin on her shoulder.

It was then that Jessica understood that he was trembling. "Are you all right? Are you hurt? What's wrong?" She was almost breathless when she finished asking him all those questions.

Meanwhile, the sound of a metal door being kicked echoed from the secret room below their feet.

"Besides the fact that I thought you were dead when I first arrived here and saw you lying on the floor after hearing an explosion?" Marcus mumbled against her ear as he hugged her tighter. "You are still bleeding. Plus, you just told me that our son is going to be a father, and we can't kill him because we are killing an innocent baby. No. I'm not okay. I need time to process this."

"We don't have time. Anna will kill him," Jessica urged, turning around to face him and putting her hand on his face. "She doesn't know his mate is pregnant. I was trying to break the curse, so we could spare his mate's life. But, I wasn't strong enough."

"Change back," Marcus requested, pulling his face away from her hand. "I don't like to look at you wearing Valentina's skin. I know that it's you beneath it, I can feel our bond, but I don't want to kiss you while you look like her."

"How do you want me to look like?" Jessica asked.

"Like yourself. Like Jessie."

Jessica nodded, closing her eyes and placing her forehead against his while reciting the words to reverse the reflection spell she had cast on herself. She didn't have time to breathe again and open her eyes to tell him that she was back to normal. Marcus kissed her and pulled her closer against his chest while using his fangs to cut his own lip and feed her with his blood.

She lost track of time as their mouths satiated the hunger for being apart. But as soon as his blood burned inside her, she broke the kiss and pulled him back so she could speak. "Marcus, I'm okay. Your blood will heal any damage I might have. But we need to follow Anna and Shane. We can't let them kill Alaric. I can't live with the death of an innocent child on my conscience."

"But we can't let him live either," Marcus declared.

"He's a monster."

"I know, trust me, I know that even better now. He is too far gone."

The vampires Jessica had broken the necks of came to life and moved their limbs. Marcus must have heard their movements because his first instinct was to secure Jessica against his chest and growl to warn them that he would bite their heads off if they were stupid enough to attack.

"Surrender or die," Marcus said, giving them a choice.

Jessica turned around, recognizing the scum she had knocked out. She had promised herself she would kill them. They were rapists and overall disgusting beings. There was no surrendering for them.

"They don't deserve to live," she declared, raising her hands and casting her fire powers against them.

Their bodies burned as they screamed in excruciating pain.

"Did they do anything bad to you?" Marcus asked.

Jessica felt the fear in his heart ripple through their mind-link. Thinking that someone could have hurt or molested her while she was there was excruciating to him.

"They would have if they were allowed to. They said they would." Turning around, she hid her face against Marcus' chest.

\* \* \*

## MARCUS

The king's attention shifted to the communicator in his ear.

"Dad, the perimeter is secure, and we have all the vampires in custody. At least, the ones who survived and surrendered," Eric warned. "Have you found Alaric yet? Is Mom alive?"

"Jessica is secured. I'm with her right now. Alaric ran away. He has secret passages that probably lead to underground tunnels. Did you put men scouting the gardens and the woods like I told you to?"

"Yes, I have. I've also called the choppers to help scout the woods. Do you need me inside? Is someone pursuing him?"

"Stay there. Anna and Shane are after him."

"I'll send more men to your location."

"I'm going after Alaric with Jessie. I'll report if I have anything new to add."

"Who are you talking to?" Jessica asked, looking up.

"Eric. He's outside monitoring all teams. Just hold on to me. We are going to follow Alaric's trail."

Jessica nodded, securing her arms around his neck.

Marcus lifted her feet from the ground and sped his way to the platform. Downstairs, he saw the destroyed door that gave access to dark descending stairs. Shane and Anika had already entered, and they would need help.

## CHAPTER TWENTY—BREAD CRUMBS

### ANNABEL

The stairs seemed to have no end. It was dark and too silent for Anna's taste. If she heard some kind of noise, other than what seemed to be bats and rats, she would understand that she was on the right track. But, maybe those stairs were there to mislead them to think Alaric was using that to run away when, in fact, he used another secret door inside the hundreds of rooms in that fortress.

"Can you hear the ocean?" Anna whispered, stopping and leaning against Shane who was just behind her.

He placed his arm around her waist and sniffed the air. "I'm smelling it, too."

"Do we have any boats securing this part of the perimeter?"

"I don't think so. The choppers are coming, though. I heard Eric talking through the earpiece before losing the signal."

"Someone is descending, fast," Anna warned, tensing and raising her sword.

"It's the king and Jessie," Shane said, nuzzling his nose against her neck. "Relax."

"Where are they?" The king asked when he arrived behind them.

"We haven't seen them yet," Shane informed.

"Move faster," he urged, passing by and speeding down.

"He's more impatient than me," Anna mumbled. "Can you keep up with us?" she asked, looking back at Shane.

"Lead the way, speedy," he joked.

Anna sped down with him behind her. When they arrived, the king and Jessie were in the middle of a cave, staring at four different tunnels that lead to unknown locations. Jessica had a fire orb hovering in the air which illuminated the space.

"What path do we choose?" Anna asked. "Are we going to split up?"

"No way," Jessie protested.

"We'll be vulnerable. Besides, we've all seen movies, it never works. We are safer together," Shane declared.

"That way," Jessie pointed out. She was aiming at the second tunnel.

"Why there?" Anna wondered.

Jessica explained, "The girl is clever. She's leaving a trail behind. There's golden fabric on the floor."

"What girl?" Marcus asked.

"Beth. She's leaving a trail to guide us."

"Or to confuse us," Shane said.

"She's a prisoner, she wants out," Anna retorted. "Myra trusts her."

"Alaric's mate is her sister. She's keen in protecting her own blood, but I saw the desperation in her eyes… I don't know who to trust right now, but if she left a trail, let's assume she wants our help."

"Let's make things easier," Shane proposed, sniffing the air. "One of these paths leads to the ocean. He may have a boat there, waiting for him to escape as a backup plan. The rest of the perimeter is surrounded by our men and there are choppers in the air, scouting the woods. Wherever these other paths may lead, if I was Alaric I would choose the path that was more likely to take me to freedom."

"So what path leads to the ocean?" Anna asked.

"The path with the golden fabric."

"Grandpa, wait!" Anna warned before he could take off and leave them behind. "Sword," she said, taking from Shane's hand the sword she had lent him, and throwing it to her grandpa. "We don't know how many men he still has with him."

"Once we are face to face with them, cover Jessie, don't leave her vulnerable," Marcus instructed. "I'll focus on Alaric. I know you wanted to have his head, Anika, but he's a lot stronger than you, and he's my problem to deal with."

Anna nodded.

"And don't kill Alaric even if you have the opportunity," Jessie added.

Arching an eyebrow, Anna asked, "Why not?"

"His mate is with child, and I wasn't able to break the curse."

"Shit!" Anna swore, rattled by the news as Shane put his hands on her shoulders so she calmed down.

"My thoughts exactly," Jessica mumbled, closing her eyes momentarily. "But we aren't monsters like him and the child is innocent."

"Then grab him and his mate alive," Anna said out loud as if she was giving instructions to herself.

Jessica secured her arms around Marcus' neck and they sped down the tunnel with her glowing orb of fire chasing after them like a sparkling fairy. Anna and Shane were left in the dark.

"Get the daggers from behind my back," Anna said to Shane. "Use the rest of the darts on them if you must. Actually, try to aim at Alaric's mate to put her to sleep. But, I don't want you fighting bare handed."

"I still have a gun," he said, showing it to her.

"A rocket launcher would be nice right about now. I mean, before Grandpa entered the tunnel, and I knew that Alaric was going to be a father. It would be a way to slow them down or blow them to pieces."

"You are kind of violent today," Shane joked, smirking at her.

Anna huffed, "He keeps getting away. It's frustrating."

"I know what you mean. Let's go before your grandpa has to face the enemy alone."

"He has Jessie. Regardless of what he might think, Jessica can take care of herself, and she has the power of imploding the damn cave if she needs to."

Anna was about to speed inside the dark tunnel when something caught her attention.

"Please, help me. Help me!"

It was a feminine voice coming from a different tunnel. It was feeble, probably from far away and just brought to their ears by the echo inside the tunnel.

Shane looked at Anna.

"It wasn't my imagination, was it?" she asked him.

He shook his head, tilting his head in the direction of the tunnel to see if he could listen again.

"Help me!"

This time, the cry for help was louder, and Anna did what was instinctive for her to do in this circumstances, she sped her way into the tunnel to aid.

*"It can be a trap,"* Shane said in their mind-link, following her close, even if she was faster than him when she was in her vampire form.

Suddenly, an explosion shook the tunnel, making dirt and small rocks fall around them. They stopped, leaning against the walls, looking up and hoping that it didn't collapse and trapped them inside.

"Something is wrong," Anna whispered, feeling the vibrations of the blast. "Do you think something happened to Grandpa and Jessie?"

"I don't know, but it's not safe to continue."

"Someone is in trouble. We need to see what's going on and save her."

"We can get trapped in this tunnel with no way to escape."

"Jessie and Grandpa can be hurt, too, but… Do you smell it?"

"Water?" Shane asked.

"Yes. There's water ahead and the sound of — rushing waves bouncing against rocks. Maybe it's an underground river."

"Help…"

"Someone is therein need of our help, probably dying because her voice is becoming weaker. We need to help her," Anna reasoned with Shane.

"I go where you go. The king can take care of himself, and I'm not leaving your side."

"We've lost too much time reasoning about acting or not," Anna sighed, grabbing his hand. "Let's move." She wrapped her arms around his torso and took him with her, so he wouldn't delay her running.

Seconds later, they arrived, stopping on the edge of the tunnel just above the rapids. The light was scarce to none existent, but Anna's sight caught a glimpse of a body behind a rock. Despite the scent of water, she could also smell blood.

"Where are you?" she called out, listening to her voice echoing inside.

"Over here…" a feminine voice replied.

Anna looked at Shane and rested her hand on his chest. "Stay here. I'm going to jump over the rocks to get her."

"I'll go," Shane protested.

"I'm the one with the feline DNA in my blood. I can also see better in the dark. I'll go, and you cover my back."

"It can be a trap."

"She's hurt. I can smell blood."

"I can also smell it, but it may not be hers. And how did she get here all by herself?"

"We'll ask her all those questions after we've saved

her."

Anna jumped, not waiting for Shane to speak again. She effortlessly floated over the rocks and landed on a rock next to the girl. "Can you move? Look at me. Are you hurt?"

The pretty vampire woman, in the wet golden dress, stared at her, moving her hands from her stomach and showing her the wound. "He stabbed me when I fought back."

"Who?"

"One of Alaric's men. I tried to delay them. I ran into this tunnel. Conrad ordered one of his men to kill me. I wasn't fast enough. He grabbed my arm and then stabbed me when I tried to fight back. We fell in the river. I was able to pull myself out with this rock. But the rapids took him away. I hope he's dead."

The girl's voice was deep and paused, though, she was experiencing pain and the bleeding didn't seem to stop. She was also soaking wet.

"What's your name?" Anna asked her.

"I'm Beth," she whispered, scowling in pain. "It stings. I think I have shards of silver inside."

"Okay, Beth, look at me. Give me your hands. I'll lean forward, and you'll grab my hands. Do you think you can do that?"

"Yes."

Anna did her best to move closer, so she could take hold of Beth's hands and grab her. She still had to jump with her over wet rocks and pray they didn't fall and get caught by the currents.

"It hurts," Beth breathed out, grabbing her stomach with one hand while the other was around Anna's shoulders.

"Shane, we need something to help pulling her up," Anna said loud enough for him to hear.

"I didn't bring a rope!"

"Use your belt."

It took a couple of minutes and some failed attempts to pull Beth back into the tunnel. Once the girl was secured, Anna was able to climb up with the help of Shane's belt.

"Who is she?" Shane asked, staring at the girl who was seated on the floor with her bloody hands pressed against her stomach.

Anna crouched in front of her. "Beth, I'm Anna and this is Shane. You are safe now. Myra told us what you did for her and how you were trapped here against your will."

Beth's eyes shone with tears. "He took my sister, Marie. I wasn't able to save her."

"The king is after Alaric. He won't get away."

"You can't kill him! My sister is pregnant, if you kill him, they will die, too."

"I know. We know that," Anna reassured her, putting her hands on her shoulders to calm her down. "We need to move you again. I know you are in pain, but we need to take you out of from this tunnel. We heard an explosion and the ceiling might collapse. Do you think you can move?"

"I'll try."

"Shane, please help me getting her up." Anna said.

Shane moved to help Beth, but she flinched. "I'm not going to hurt you," Shane assured. "Just put your arm around my neck."

After a while, Beth was walking on her two legs, and Anna and Shane found their way outside the tunnel, even if it was at a painfully slow speed while Anna pressed on Beth's wound to keep the bleeding under control.

## CHAPTER TWENTY-ONE—BETRAYAL

### ALARIC

"Conrad, bring Beth," Alaric ordered, grabbing Marie after the platform lowered into the level below them. Moments after, his trusty number one appeared beside him, holding Marie's sister.

Looking at the wall before him, he waited until his men moved one of the shelves, so they could access the secret passage behind it. After opening the steel reinforced door, they proceed to descend the narrow staircase carved in the rock. The sound of the door closing and being locked assured him that even if someone followed them there, the door would hold them until they had time to escape.

Alaric hadn't survived this long without being paranoid enough to have several escape plans. He didn't know how they had found them—or even who they were—but he was ready to flee. He could figure out who was coming for him later. Now, he needed to take his mate to safety since they were still bonded, and all that happened to her would happen to him. She was a liability, and he had to secure her. The ritual should have worked. They should have been unbound. There was no time to think about a plausible reason for it not working, though.

To increase his annoyance, Marie was slower since

she was pregnant. In return, he was slower, too. It rattled his nerves and made him growl all the way down the uneven stairs into the secret caves under the fortress. Behind him, he could hear Beth trying to fight Conrad. He was in no mood to deal with one of her tantrums.

He yelled at her, "Beth, they will kill us if you keep fighting Conrad. Move and stop delaying us!"

They were outnumbered. He only had four more bodyguards to protect them, not including Conrad because he needed his new number one to secure Beth.

"Which way, master?" one of the vampires in the front asked Alaric when they arrived at the caves.

There were four different tunnels to choose from.

Alaric instructed, "We need to take the second tunnel. It will lead us to the sea where I have a boat to safely take us to a submarine."

"How did you have time to call a submarine?" Marie asked out of breath.

"I was already planning to leave after all the rituals were over," Alaric clarified. "I have friends in Europe who can help us, and I have other men in my castle, waiting for us."

"No, no," Beth protested.

Alaric glared back and witnessed her trying to escape Conrad's hold. "Beth, don't force my hand. I'm not in the mood. Your sister and I are in danger. You need to behave if you want the baby to survive."

"You want to kill our baby," Marie spat, holding onto her belly. "Liar!"

"Let's go," Alaric ordered, ignoring his mate's glare

and moving forward.

Dragging Marie in the process, he entered the second tunnel.

"Stop! I can't walk this fast!" Marie begged as she pulled her arms from his hold.

He stopped and released her, ready to slap her. "Shut up! It's your fault that I can't move faster. You were the one who had to get pregnant and ruin my plans."

* * *

**MARIE**

Marie flinched and squinted when he raised his hand to hit her. Nothing happened, though.

Sneering, he said as she opened her eyes, "I can't have you fainting in here. Just follow me."

Marie bowed in compliance as she grabbed the skirt of her dress so she wouldn't stumble on the rocky ground. Her body was sore and feeble. Every time she breathed, the air burned her lungs. In her condition, she needed to be carried.

"Are you coming or what?" Alaric asked her.

Tilting back her head, she called, "Conrad." He had been Marie's personal bodyguard before he was promoted to his new position.

"Why the hell are you calling him for? He's busy with your sister. Now, stop delaying us all and come!" Alaric ordered. "Move," he said to the vampire in front of them.

Before Marie could blink, Alaric grabbed her wrist

and dragged her a few feet.

"Master," Conrad called.

Marie looked back and saw him, holding Beth, as the other two of his men waited to enter the tunnel.

Alaric came to a halt and turned around, releasing Marie. "What is it now?" he asked, clearly upset by Conrad causing them to be delayed. "Do you honestly want to stay behind and face whoever is chasing us?"

"Take Beth," Conrad ordered one of the remaining vampire bodyguards. "I'll help the mistress," he said, walking to Marie and putting an arm around her waist.

She sighed in relief when Conrad secured her and helped her stand up.

"I'm tired and my skin still burns from the ritual," she told him as he rubbed her back.

"That's not what I ordered you to do!" Alaric yelled as his eyes turned red. "We have no time for this shit! They are right behind us, and we will get ourselves killed if we don't move on!"

As if on cue, thumping sounds and metal clankings were heard as someone tried to kick down the reinforced door upstairs.

Time was running out, Marie was aware of that. So, ignoring her mate, she urged Conrad, "Do it now."

Conrad nodded and yelled at the vampire holding Beth, "Kill the whore!"

Marie smirked as Alaric shouted in return, "Don't touch her! I'll fucking kill you if you touch her!"

"Grab him while he's weak," Marie told Conrad.

Marie's attention was caught by her sister as she

witnessed Beth kick the vampire in his private parts, after struggling to get free. With the vampire doubling over, Beth was able to run away into a different tunnel.

"What the hell is going on?" Alaric asked since another of Conrad's men had grabbed him and immobilized him, preventing him from helping Beth.

"You are no longer in a position to tell anyone what to do," Marie informed him as she walked to him and stabbed a needle in his neck.

"What are you doing? Marie..." Alaric's voice faded away as weakness took possession of his limbs.

"Saving my baby," she indulged him in a response as she smiled. The exhilaration of victory washed over her for what was happening.

Before his eyes closed, and he fell into a slumber, Alaric managed to ask, "What did you do to me?"

Ignoring Alaric, Marie's eyes shifted to Conrad. "I want her dead!"

Conrad nodded as he ordered the vampire who had let Beth escape, "Go after her and kill her,"

Marie focused her hearing on the pounding sound coming from upstairs. "They will find us here if we don't move."

"Mistress, what do you want me to do with him?" Conrad asked as he pointed at Alaric.

"Take him with us. We are still bonded. We can't use the boat or the submarine. Those men are loyal to him. We need to go somewhere secure."

"I have everything ready for us," Conrad said to her as he placed his hand on her belly. "No one will hurt you or the baby, mistress."

"Good," she whispered, laying her hand on his face. "Lead the way."

"Hold on to me." Conrad grabbed her in his arms. "Follow me!" he ordered the remaining men as he sped his way out of the tunnel.

## CHAPTER TWENTY-TWO — THE EXPLOSION

### JESSICA

When Marcus reached the end of the tunnel, he stopped and put Jessica on the ground, behind him. She peeked around him and saw a high ledge overlooking a small beach under the cave with an opening to the sea.

They hid against the walls of the tunnel as Marcus appeared to assess the place and the threat.

"Are you seeing Alaric?" Jessica asked him, holding on to his arm. She rested her head against his back, inhaling his scent. She had missed him terribly. It was nice to be able to touch him again.

Marcus replied, "I'm not seeing him. There are just three men in a small boat. We may be in the wrong tunnel."

"It's an escape route. Why else would they have a boat here? They must be waiting for Alaric. But...how could we get here before he did?"

"Maybe he had already left, and they are just waiting for other survivors," Marcus assumed.

"He's not that far ahead of us but...he could have taken another tunnel. We should go back."

"Where are Anna and Shane?" Marcus asked, looking back.

"They were just behind us," Jessica mumbled, turning around and pouting her lips as she squinted at the darkness inside the tunnel. "Maybe they saw something we didn't. I don't like this."

"We need to grab those men and interrogate them."

After Marcus spoke, the sound of a helicopter flying over the sea echoed inside the cave.

"Kevin is here," Marcus said.

Spinning around, she asked, "Where?"

Marcus pointed at the openings in the caves where the waves were bashing against the rock. "In the helicopter. They found the caves. I have reception here."

"Tell him to search for a boat," Jessica said. "We'll take down those two vampires."

Marcus nodded and added, "He heard you."

"We should…" her words got stuck in her throat when she realized the vampires in the boat were shouting orders to grab weapons and annihilate the threat.

"What are they doing?" Jessica asked, widening her eyes when she noticed that they were heavily armed and were aiming a rocket at the helicopter that poured a spotlight inside the cave. "They are going to blow up the chopper!"

Without thinking, she ran towards the beach, right into the enemy's line of fire. Kevin's life was in danger. In the background, she heard her mate yelling her name.

Jessica flared a wave of fire around her body as she ran in the enemy's direction. They saw her and pointed their automatic guns at her. Yet, they managed to launch the rocket.

The witch stretched her arms forward and opened her

hands, surrounding the missile with her kinetic powers and preventing it from leaving the cave. She heard the sound of guns being fired. She sensed the air around her being disturbed by bullets, but her fire was preventing them from reaching her, melting down the metal and exploding the gunpowder. However, the rocket was trying to escape the cocoon of energy she had placed around it. Closing her eyes, she focused harder as the missile exploded inside her force field, shaking the cave and creating a shockwave that made her fly back and hit the rocky walls.

"Marcus..." she breathed out. Her head was throbbing hard, her ears ringing, and the inside of her mouth tasted like blood. She opened her eyes but saw nothing. Everything seemed dark and quiet around her. Eventually, she passed out.

\* \* \*

## MARCUS

"Jessie..." Marcus called as he kneeled beside her and put his hands around her face. "Honey..." Marcus' voice was weak. His heart raced and his body quivered.

He hadn't been fast enough to grab her before she hit the wall. He had killed all the vampires, but he wasn't fast enough to save her before the blast.

Everything around them was surrounded by a cloud of smoke, making it hard for him to breathe. The tunnel had been partially obstructed by the falling rocks and there were no signs of Alaric or his men. But all that was troubling him, at the moment, was that Jessica could be dead.

The king's hands kept trembling. His eyes closed as he lightly brushed his fingers across Jessie's face. He wanted to scream her name, but it wouldn't help his situation. It wouldn't bring her back to him. So, he mumbled her name over and over again like a prayer.

His senses were still affected by the blast. He couldn't hear properly, but his sense of smell told him that she was bleeding. The good news was that she had a pulse. Running his fingers through her hair, he noticed the blood damping the back of her head. She still had his blood in her system. Even if she died, she would return as a vampire. But Jessica didn't want to be a vampire. Not just yet. Every minute he wasted there, grieving and blaming himself, was pointless. She needed a doctor. He took her in his arms and sped his way out, hoping the tunnel was still intact, and he would be able to reach the house.

* * *

## ANNABEL

Anna and Shane arrived at the top of the stairs when they heard the sound of something speeding behind them. Shane immediately turned back and aimed his gun to the dark.

"Jessica needs a doctor!" Marcus warned before

stopping in front of Shane's gun. "Who's that?"

Beth was in Anna's arms, unconscious.

"One of Alaric's prisoners," Shane explained.

"My earpiece isn't working. We need a doctor," Marcus told him.

"There are medics outside the house," Anna informed him. "I'm taking Beth there, too."

"Lead the way then," Marcus urged.

Moments later, Anna and Marcus were laying both women on the stretchers.

"What happened inside? We heard a blast!" Anna asked her grandfather. "How did Jessica get hurt?"

"We'll talk about this later," he said, following Jessica's stretcher.

"Your Majesty, we need you to stay back while we take her vitals signs," one of the doctors told him while listening to her heart.

"She's alive, isn't she?" he asked, grief haunting his expression.

"She's alive. Her heart is beating. She may have internal bleeding, though. The wound on the back of her head looks bad," the doctor shared. "But we need space to work on her."

"I gave her vampire blood. Do you think she needs more?"

"The blood must be healing her, and we have a needle ready for her if she needs more," the doctor confirmed.

As if on cue, a nurse arrived with a needle that the doctor administered to her arm.

"She'll be okay," Anna said, placing her hand on her grandfather's shoulder.

"Where's Eric?" Marcus asked, after staying silent for a moment, staring at Jessica's face, and following the doctors and nurses' movements around her.

"He's leading a team in the woods," Sebastien said, arriving with a worried expression. "His communicator is off. What happened to Jessica?"

"She'll be fine," the king mumbled, stepping back when the doctor urged him to let them do his job, once again. "She hit her head...but she'll be fine."

Anna noticed the king's trembling hands and pale face. She could only imagine what he felt. Jessie was her best friend, she was also worried about her, but she had the misfortune of seeing how her departure had affected him. "Grandpa, one way or another, she'll live," she stated.

His eyes were somber when he looked at her. "She didn't want to be one of us just yet. I should have been faster."

"It's not your fault."

The king gritted his teeth and with narrowed eyes, he asked Sebastien. "How many of Alaric's men were you able to imprison? Did anyone see Alaric? We weren't able to find him. He had vanished."

Sebastien rubbed the back of his head as he reported what he had seen. "There were a lot of casualties, but we still managed to take twenty men alive. There's also a crazy amount of prisoners in his dungeons. The majority being girls...human girls who provided blood and... Let's just say it's not pretty down there. We have people taking care of them, but many are too scared to trust us. I had to leave. I was beginning to feel extremely sick. The state of those girls..."

Marcus' attention was drawn to Jessica's when she started to cough. He flew to her side, grabbing her hand and ignoring Sebastien's report.

"Jessie..."

"I think she'll be fine," the doctor said, checking her vitals again and opening her eyes to see how she reacted to the light. "She seems to be regaining consciousness."

"Jessie, can you hear me?"

"We still need to take her to a hospital. She needs a CAT scan."

"Do we have time to wait to arrive in town?" Marcus asked, looking at the doctor.

"I have connections in several hospitals. We shouldn't wait that long."

"We'll take a chopper. Alert the nearest hospital then."

The doctor nodded as he rushed to the ambulance and picked up his cell phone.

"I'll ask Kevin to send down a chopper," Sebastien said as he pressed on his earpiece.

"Thank you," the king said, letting out a breath of relief. "Anna," the king called his granddaughter. "How's the girl you found doing?"

Beth's stretcher wasn't far from Jessica's.

"She'll live," she said as the paramedics removed shards of silver from her wound. Beth appeared to have fainted.

"Okay. I need to fly to the hospital with Jessie."

"I want to go with you," Anna said, approaching Jessie's stretcher and holding her hand. "Can she hear us?"

"I'm trying to tap into her mind but...I can't hear her thoughts."

"Jessie, just be strong," Anna demanded, leaning down and kissing her cheek.

"I need you to stay behind. I need you to help Shane and Sebastien with the prisoners and the girls that were found in the dungeons."

"But Grandpa, I want to be with Jessie, too. She's my best friend."

"I'll call you as soon as she opens her eyes."

Anna put her hands on her hips and looked past the garden into the woods. "Then, I should be out there with Eric, looking for Alaric."

"He's long gone. I'm not saying that we shouldn't be looking for him, but he vanished in the underground caves. Shane can assemble teams to search the other tunnels. Right now, I need you here to help."

"Fine," Anna nodded. "Maybe Beth knows something. I'll bring her to our home to debrief her."

"I have to go," the king said, staring at the place in the garden where there was enough space for a chopper to land.

"Marcus," Jessie called his name, grabbing his hand when two men began to move her stretcher.

"Jessie," Marcus leaned down, placing a hand on her

face and looking at her closed eyes. She slowly opened her eyes, blinking several times. "I'm sorry...for being reckless. I didn't want them to kill Kevin."

"That's okay, baby. Just promise me you won't give up, that you'll fight to stay alive. We still need to have a lot of babies before you turn into a vampire."

Jessica tried to smirk and nodded. "Okay," she whispered.

"We need to go," the doctor urged.

Marcus nodded, placing a kiss on Jessica's lips. "I'll be right beside you."

"Your Majesty," the doctor called.

Marcus raised his eyes to stare at the doctor.

"You're bleeding, sir."

With all the commotion and worries, it seemed the king hadn't even noticed that the vampires had wounded him.

Anna rushed to his side and looked down. She touched his torso, sensing the blood soaking his clothes. "He's wounded on his right side near his hip."

"I can remove the bullet in the chopper," the doctor told her.

Marcus nodded and moved forward, following the stretcher that was carrying Jessica to the helicopter.

## CHAPTER TWENTY-THREE—NEW BEGINNINGS

### ANNABEL

It had been a long night and an even longer day. Anna was resting her eyes, seated on the couch, near the hospital bed where Beth's sleeping body was resting.

Even after they had taken out the silver shards, the girl was still too weak to wake up. She wanted to talk to her and ask her what she knew concerning Alaric's whereabouts. Beth could have overheard a conversation about where he might be heading to.

Eric and Shane had been left at Alaric's hideout, scouting the woods and the tunnels under the house's foundations. She had been worried about Jessica, only relaxing once her grandfather called, telling her that Jessica was awake and healing fast. She had a concussion and needed to stay in the hospital a little longer, but the scans showed that she didn't seem to have any physical or psychological damage. She had some broken bones, but they had healed with the help of the vampire blood.

Meanwhile, Beth had silver dust in her bloodstream and it was preventing her from healing completely. The doctor had said it was just a matter of time for her to start healing herself since she was a pureblood vampire and should heal faster than the rest of the vampires. But, Annabel was intrigued by the bruises and the scars on her body that weren't healing. Beth had all the signs of being abused and tortured.

She dreaded the idea of finding out everything the vampire had experienced because it would make her sick to her stomach. She would want to go after Alaric and kill him over and over again, together with every single one of his men.

"Marie…"

It was the fourth time Beth was whispering that name while sleeping and moving as if she was experiencing a nightmare. Anna grabbed her hand to calm her down, whispering reassuring words, and caressing her face. It made her less agitated.

Annabel's phone rang. She got up and picked it up as she headed to the hallway. "Yes?"

"There's no sign of him," Shane said on the other side. "Eric is on his way there. He wants to check on the prisoners. Where are you?"

Resting her back against the wall, she answered, "I'm in the medical compound with Beth. I didn't want to leave her alone. Besides, she might wake up and tell us something useful."

"How's she's doing?"

"She's stable. It's strange, she should be healing already. She's reacting more like a human than a pureblood vampire."

"We don't know what she has experienced and how psychologically damaged she is."

"Dulce said Myra told her that Beth was on our side. She killed Vincent and made it possible for us to find Alaric's hideout. I'm going to stay with her and make sure she heals."

"Okay, honey. Meanwhile, I think you should know that…"

"What?" Anna asked, frowning at the delay in finishing the sentence.

"Jessica and the king…left."

Her voice couldn't conceal her shock. "Where?"

"The king wants to spend time with Jessica."

"They ran away!" Anna said breathlessly as she paced around the corridor. "How can they be so reckless? We are looking for Alaric. Francesco and his evil vixen mate are still at the palace, waiting for Jessica to get back. The flower arrangements and the food are spoiling in the kitchen. I have victims and prisoners filling our compounds. I really don't need Jessica and my grandfather running away like two teenagers with the intention of marrying in some cheesy church in Las Vegas!"

"Hum…breathe deep and try to relax," Shane suggested with a sweet, placating voice.

"Honey!"

"I know, but we can donate the food… The flowers can decorate the palace. I'm here. Eric is here. We'll take care of everything. And they aren't eloping. The king felt he needed to spend some time alone with Jessica. Marriage can wait, and I don't think the king wants Jessica to go home just yet and see everything that is going on there."

Anna sat on the floor and calmed herself down, looking at the white wall. Shane was always a lot more reasonable than her. His soft voice and relaxed point of view made her feel a lot better. "Is she fully healed?"

"Jessica? I think so. I didn't see her. I just talked with the king."

"She could have come here, so I could make sure that she was okay."

"I know, baby. But, don't worry about them. I believe the king is still frightened by the idea that he could have lost her. They need time to talk about why she left the way she did and about what happened when she was a prisoner."

"Fine. What should I do about King Francesco and his entourage?"

"Eric will take care of that. I hope..." Shane said on the other side.

Anna rolled her eyes, feeling frustrated. Then, with a sweet voice, she added, "Just come back home. I miss you, and I don't like knowing you are there without me."

"I'll be home soon. We are just packing everything to leave. How are things there?"

"Sebastien and Dulce are taking care of the girls. The majority of them were beaten and malnourished. We hope to find out their names and, after treating them, find their families."

"I'll help with that as soon as I get back. My officers can help in finding their families and search their names in the missing person's database."

"Okay. I'm going to try and get some rest."

"Okay. I love you. I'll be back soon."

"I love you, too."

Anna hung up and headed to Beth's bedroom. She dropped her sore body onto the couch next to a small table where she put her phone down. With a resigned sigh, she rubbed her temples due to her head hurting from the lack of sleep. Then, she closed her eyes and let sleep bring some peace to her mind and body.

* * *

**BETH**

Beth woke up screaming. She looked around to where she was and saw the girl who had saved her rush to her side.

Anna asked with a worried expression, "What's wrong?"

Blinking several times, Beth fisted her hands on the bedding. "I had a nightmare. Where am I?"

"You are safe. You are in a medical facility underneath my grandfather's palace. We brought you here after you fainted."

She nodded as she looked at the white walls and then at herself. "I need to shower…"

"Yes, you do. I have brought clean clothes for you to change into. It's also about time we remove that from your neck."

Beth touched the collar Anna pointed at.

"He's a beast for treating you like an animal," Anna muttered, clearly upset.

Tears welled up in her eyes as her breathing became erratic with the memories of what she had endured.

"This doesn't feel real."

"What doesn't feel real?"

"Being free."

Anna sat on her bed. "I can't even imagine what you suffered through. But this is real, and you are safe now."

Beth nodded as she rested her back against the headboard of the hospital bed. "He managed to escape, didn't he?"

"He did. We were wondering if you knew where he was planning to go next."

"He mentioned a submarine waiting to take us to Europe where he had friends who could help us. He mentioned his castle. I had been in that fortress since he kidnapped my sister and me, so I have no idea where his castle is."

"That's a really good lead," Anna said with a happy voice as Beth looked at her pretty face. "I'm going to call…" Beth grabbed Anna's hand before she could leave her side.

"The nightmare isn't over yet, is it? Do you think he believes I'm dead?"

"I have no idea." Anna sat back on the bed. "Do you think he'll come back to get you if he finds out you are alive? Didn't he tell his man to kill you?"

"No, it wasn't him. He's mad, but he doesn't want to kill me." Beth paused as she gulped with the painful memory. "It was Marie who ordered my death…"

"Your own sister! Why?"

Staring at the gray blanket, she explained, "Everything is very confusing. Alaric didn't want them to hurt me because he has a delusional fixation on me. He wanted the witch to bind our souls together."

"I thought he wanted her to break his curse."

"That too. But something went wrong because the witch couldn't break the curse."

"When we first met, you said that Conrad had ordered his man to kill you, not Maric."

Beth nodded. "That's what is strange. Marie ordered Conrad, and he disobeyed Alaric. I ran, and I hope they believe I'm dead. Things between Alaric and Mary seemed tense... I just hope he doesn't kill the baby."

Anna held Beth's hand in hers. "He has no idea that you survived and, if Alaric is still cursed, he won't risk his life by threatening your sister's life. Vampire women become vulnerable when they are pregnant, fragile like humans. You need to have faith."

Beth nodded as she brushed away the tears that escaped down her cheeks.

"You are too nice, Beth. You are afraid for your sister and baby's life even after she wanted to kill you."

"She's not thinking straight. She's mad with jealousy, and Alaric has been a monster to both of us."

Anna got up and rolled her shoulders. "You should remove those clothes and have a shower. I'll help you take that thing off," she said, pointing at the collar. "Then, while you bathe, I'll get you more blood to see if you heal faster this time."

"Are we here all by ourselves. Where are the rest of the prisoners? He had a lot of girls trapped in his dungeon. Were they saved?"

"Yes, don't worry about anything. We have another facility they were taken to."

"Why am I not there?"

"You aren't human. You need a different type of attention."

Beth nodded. "I see... But I'm not your prisoner, am I? I can leave after answering your questions and am healed?"

"No, Beth, you are not our prisoner. We know you were a victim. Come. I'll help you if you are still too weak."

"Thank you," Beth said as she took her hand.

After the hot shower, Beth got dressed in a pair of leggings and a sweater. She wiped the steam from the bathroom mirror and stared at her pale expression while her hair fell about her shoulders. She looked like crap. Sighing, she dried the remaining water from her hair before leaving the bedroom.

"How are you feeling?" Anna asked from the double-seat gray couch next to the entrance.

Beth walked to her and sat down. "I'm still weak."

"The bruises haven't healed yet," Anna mumbled, touching a few purple marks around Beth's neck.

Beth recoiled, closing her eyes in pain.

"You should try drinking blood."

"My stomach is upset. I have been throwing up everything I drink."

"The doctor gave you a blood transfusion while you were being moved here. It didn't seem to work. Maybe we should try another one now that you are awake."

"I'm feeling better after a shower. How long did I sleep for?"

Anna looked at her watch. "Eight hours."

"So it's morning," she whispered as she hugged herself and looked at the white tile.

"What is still troubling you?"

Beth confessed, "I have no idea where to go after getting better."

"Don't you have any family?"

"It's just me and Marie."

"Well, you can stay with us while you recover. Then, it's up to you. You will be safer living in our town. We can find you a home and a job. Do you have a mate?"

Beth shook her head. "Who would possibly want me after what has happened?"

"Let's not talk about that. You have your life back."

She shrugged. "I guess that's true."

"Beth, you survived hell. With the information you gave us, we are closer to catching Alaric and saving your sister and her baby. You can't lose hope."

"I've spent so much time thinking about escaping that I have no idea what to do now that I'm free."

The sound of a door opening echoed throughout the empty compound.

"I asked Rose to bring us a fresh jar of blood while you were showering," Anna informed.

Beth was about to nod, but, suddenly, as if a heavy wave crashed over her, her body stiffened and her senses went into overdrive.

"What's wrong?"

"I'm not sure. I feel some kind of energy…" Beth said, staring at her hands, noticing how they were shaking in response to the change of energy around her.

Her heart raced inside her chest as her nostrils scouted the air, trying to figure out why the scent of wood and citrines felt so irresistible. It was enticing and made her fangs appear in her mouth. Beth covered her mouth, feeling flustered by her conflicting reactions.

"I'm feeling," she whispered, breathless, her vision blurring and shivers descending down her spine, "a pull…"

Footsteps echoed in the compound and, before Beth could control herself, she sped into the hallway.

* * *

## ANNABEL

Anna's focused her attention on Beth when her pupils dilated and her cheeks turned red as if life was returning to her, or she was going to have a seizure.

"Are you going to have some kind of heart attack?" Anna asked. "Beth?" She didn't answer and kept sniffing the hair as if enthralled by a scent.

Footsteps echoed in the corridor. Before Anna could get her back to bed, Beth sped from the bedroom and out the door.

"Beth!" Anna called, unsure of what was happening. She seemed too weak to be able to do that.

Anna decided to follow her, only to stop in the middle of the hallway and see Eric and Beth face to face. Eric's eyes were wide opened, shining purple in his vampire form. *What the hell was going on?*

Beth screamed, turned around, and ran away from Eric. Anna sensed her passing by. Then, her uncle sped behind the girl.

"Uncle? Don't scare the girl!" Anna shouted, but they were long gone, running to the far end of the compound where the holding cells for prisoners were. They were all empty because the prisoners were in some other compound.

When Anna caught them, Beth was locked in one of the holding cells, leaning against the wall, the farthest she could get from Eric who was immobilized outside, looking at her.

"What the hell is going on?" Anna asked, stopping beside him. "Why are you chasing our guest?"

"Who is she?" he asked, flustered and breathless. He didn't look at Anna. It seemed that his eyes were caught by the sight of the frightened girl, hiding her face against her knees and sobbing in the corner of the holding cell.

"That's Beth, she was… Wait, why did she run from you?"

"I have no idea. I'm not trying to hurt her… It's just that…"

"What?" Anna asked, noticing his dazed expression.

"She's my mate," he breathed out, leaning closer to the bars.

"Don't touch it," Anna warned, pulling him back.

"They are made of silver. You'll get burned in the process. What do you mean with *she's your mate*?"

"She knows it, too. Why did she run? Let me get in…"

"No!" Anna stopped him, holding him by his coat and pulling him back. "Just…get out of here. Let me talk to Beth."

"She's my mate! I won't move an inch. I want to talk to her."

"Fuck!" Anna cursed. "Let me talk to her first. You have no idea what's going through her head right now, but you look too much like Alaric at first sight."

"And why is that a problem?" Eric's voice trembled. "Where was she found?"

"I think you know that answer already."

Eric's eyes lost their shine. He stepped back as if hit by an energy that made him feel dizzy. "He hurt her, didn't he? He hurt…my…mate."

Anna placed one hand behind his back and the other over his chest. She felt that she needed to balance him because the emotional shock was taking its toll on Eric.

"Beth," Anna called the girl, listening to her weep. "Beth, this isn't Alaric. Look at him. Please, look at him."

Beth kept mumbling incoherently while rocking her body back and forward.

"Let me go to her," Eric begged.

Anna held him still, preventing him from entering the holding cell.

"She's my mate, Anna! I want to go to her. I…" He lost his voice, and she noticed his eyes were shining with unshed tears.

"Let me talk to her first, Uncle. You need to be patient. She's been through a lot and needs…to understand that we don't want to hurt her and that you aren't him."

His voice came out shaky and, at the same time, powered by anger. "I'll kill him, Anna! I will. I can't believe he had her. He hurt her!"

Anna placed both hands on his face, wiping away the tears that rolled down his cheeks. "I promise you that he will pay. But you need to let me talk to her. You need to control your anger so you won't scare her even more."

Eric nodded, placing his own hands over hers. "How could he do this?"

"I doubt he knew she was your mate. But he's a sadist. You'll need to be patient."

Eric nodded again, raising his head to stare at his weeping mate. Anna could only imagine what went on inside his mind when his body trembled as he clenched his hands into fists and took deep breaths to calm his rage. New tears fell down his cheeks.

## CHAPTER TWENTY-FOUR — BONDING


### JESSICA

The sunlight was pouring into the bedroom, announcing the existence of life outside those walls. Jessica stretched her arms up in the air while wrapped inside Marcus' shirt. She smiled and opened the balcony doors, stepping outside to face the view.

"I love it out here," she whispered, turning her head to watch Marcus, half-covered with the sheet on the bed, showing his perfect torso and amazing smile. Her stomach bubbled with happiness. "After we buy clothes, I want to see everything."

From the balcony of their hotel suite, Jessica could see the Prague Castle, the Charles Bridge, the Dancing House, and a lot of other monuments in Prague she couldn't wait to visit.

"It's chilly outside. Come back to bed, love. We'll order breakfast and then we can go out shopping for new clothes."

Jessica spun around after closing the doors. Then, she ran to the bed and jumped on it, showing how happy she was. Marcus embraced her and kissed her nose, her forehead, and then her lips while she giggled.

Jessica asked him as she caressed his face, "How long are we staying here?"

"How long do you want to stay?"

"We could visit Amsterdam in a couple of days. I've never been there. It's supposed to be beautiful, too. When was the last time you were in Europe?"

"It's been…ages. Everything looks different," he whispered, sitting her on his lap and running his hand up her thigh.

"I was thinking that we could go to Australia on our honeymoon. Have you ever been to Australia?"

"Once, a long time ago. Speaking about the wedding, we should call Anna. She must be worried about you. They tried to call us last night."

"She's fine and knows that I'm fine. She should let her grandparents have some fun."

Marcus smirked. "We have lots of fun."

"If we return home, we'll have a lot of drama, a lot of crying about the fact Alaric escaped, and a lot of stuff to deal with because of Valentina's evil doings. Speaking of which, I wonder what Francesco did to her."

"He should lock her up in a mental institution. I pity him. His mate was planning to betray him."

"She holds a grudge against him. She's a raving lunatic."

"Forget about other people's problems. Our immediate problem is what we shall order for breakfast," Marcus said, kissing her shoulder and nuzzling his nose against her cleavage. "I'm not sure if I want to go outside. I've missed you, and you are too irresistible to let go of."

Jessica giggled. "Are we being selfish?"

Her voice was sober and her face became solemn

when she lifted her head to look into his eyes.

Marcus lost his smile and shook his head. "No, we are not being selfish. I've almost lost you again. Alaric may have escaped, but you are still alive. We have a whole life ahead of us. We need to make new memories. We need to get to know each other all over again. I'm excited about it. But you are right. At home, we would have to deal with a lot of drama that would ruin our present happiness. And if we are being selfish, so be it. I want you all to myself. Our children and grandchildren can wait. And if the end of the world is near, it can also wait. We have a city to explore, new clothes to buy, and a lot of babies to make."

Jessica smiled. "A lot of babies to make?"

Marcus nodded.

"I love you," she whispered, feeling emotional about the happiness of being there with him and their plans for the future.

"I love you, too."

Marcus brushed his fingers along her cheek, carefully taking her chin between his fingers, and placing his lips on her plump mouth to kiss. He pressed their lips together tenderly. Hugging her, he turned her around and placed her under his body.

Jessica's giggle was muffled as she snaked her arms around his neck and kissed him harder. As much as she enjoyed the dreams of them together, she had to confess, the real thing was a lot better. Their love had survived death, reincarnation, and even the test of time. Now they were together, nothing could stop them from being happy again.

# EPILOGUE—KARMA

## ALARIC

The place where Alaric was being held captive brought him memories of a time he had been isolated in his father's palace. They had locked him up, starved him to near death, and claimed they were doing that for his own good. They wanted to cleanse him from his bloodlust. A long time ago, he had found a way to escape that awful place to have his revenge. Though, he had been a lot more comfortable in his own private quarters of his childhood home than in a smelly, dampened, and dark dungeon.

Everybody would pay for their betrayal. Somehow he was going to free himself and then the ones who put him here would pay with their own lives, even his cunning and manipulative mate who had fooled him into believing that she was weak and scared. Marie had earned some new respect from him after her disloyalty. Somehow, she had convinced one of his most loyal men into obeying her orders and betraying his master. It was a sneaky thing to do. Marie wasn't as weak as he first thought.

As for Conrad, he was going to have a slow death. He would peel and dismember him in front of Marie, after displaying her guts to the ravens.

The only reason he was alive was because Marie

would die if he died. The reason why he was feeling weaker and weaker was because Marie had not been feeding him blood. He was simply left there, unconscious, for days that he hadn't counted. But if she continued to ignore him, she would suffer, too. They were still connected. By some unexplained reason, the curse wasn't lifted. The witch had tried…Valentina. Not her, Jessica wearing Valentina's appearance. She had tried to break the curse and failed.

Between the moments of clarity and madness, he continued to remember that Beth might be dead. It hurt him thinking he would never see her again. She had fled. She was smart. Maybe she was able to survive. He wasn't so smart… He didn't realize that Conrad was under Marie's spell.

*Was he in love with her? Was he stupid enough to think that Marie loved him in return?*

But only love could explain the betrayal. Love or greed.

*What did she promise him?*

He had more moments of madness than sanity. He needed to feed. He needed to tap into other people's memories and emotions to survive. The craving was unbearable.

The sound of a door opening made him open his eyes and stare at the dark wall. Someone was coming down the stairs. He followed the footsteps, evaluating the gentle step and the rhythm of the female coming down. A faint smell of roses came to his nose, taunting him and reminding him of the tantalizing taste of her blood. Even if he hated her, he loved her, too. Maybe he could reason with her and convince her to let him go. She was weak, and she wanted to believe that he could love her as she loved him. Despite all that he had done to her, Marie loved him.

"Why did you betray me?" he asked when she stopped at a safe distance from his holding cell.

"You wanted to kill our baby. I couldn't let you do that. I love my baby, and I want to have it."

Her voice was weak and her smell was enticing. He fought the urge to jump against the silver bars and growl at her like a mad animal inside a cage. He was going to pretend to be rational. Not that he wasn't... He was rational. He was also mad and would rip her throat out if he was an arm's length of her pretty neck.

"What did you tell Conrad for him to betray me?" Alaric folded his arms over his chest, musing on the ceiling and refusing to look at her.

"We are in love. He knew you wanted to harm me. With you here, we can be together."

"You don't love him. I know you don't. I would know if you loved someone else but me, and I would hurt you for that."

"There's a lot about me that you don't know because you never cared to find out. I can control what I want you to see in my head, in my memories... I tried to make you happy, but I can't understand your obsession for Beth. I won't understand, and I won't let you bind her soul to ours. I'm your only mate. You won't have anyone else."

"So…all this is happening because you are jealous of Beth?"

"Not only because of that. You are mad, Alaric. You hurt everybody, and you are evil. You wanted to hurt our child."

He sat on his uncomfortable bed. "So…this is you…protecting me?"

"Not you. Protecting my baby."

"If I let you keep the baby…"

"Don't," Marie ordered with renewing power in her voice. "I just came here to tell you that as long as I am pregnant, you'll stay here. I won't harm you because it would be harming me. However, I have no intention of letting you be free. You are a threat to yourself, whether you realize it or not."

"Are you going to starve me to death? Because I need to eat, Marie!" he screamed, leaning forward and glaring at her with his red eyes. His words startled her and made her recoil further. "Pathetic! Where's your lover who should face me? You are shaking like a little girl."

"Shut up!" Marie fisted her hands. "I just came to see if you were better after a few days without blood. But I see you are still the same bastard."

Marie turned around to leave.

"Wait!" Alaric pleaded, moving to the bars and holding on to them. His hands were burned, and Marie screamed in pain while he smirked at her. "You should have thought better about this…silly girl."

Marie straightened her shoulders and turned to face him. "Soon enough, silver won't harm you anymore. I'm becoming human, the baby is growing inside of me, and you'll experience the same things as me." Marie smirked. "I hope you enjoy your new room. It's a lot better than the one you placed me in when we first met."

"Tell me something before you leave," Alaric demanded, swallowing his pride and concealing the hate that was burning inside his soul.

"What do you want to know?"

"Did you kill Beth?"

Marie's eyes turned black and her fangs came out. She hissed at him. "She's rotting in hell. I ripped her heart from her chest and then left her body for the wild animals!"

"You are lying…" Alaric said, aware of the hate and jealousy lacing her words.

Marie smirked wickedly. "Am I? I guess you'll never know. Enjoy your eternity in this hell hole. This is the last time you'll see me. From now on, you will only have your caretaker and the endless solitude and silence to keep you company. I won't let you starve because I need you healthy to have this baby, but I have no intentions of spending my life, dealing with your madness and your lack of love for me. Conrad and I are free from you, and my baby will have a new father."

Marie grabbed the front of her dress, raising it to make it easier to walk. Lifting her head proudly, she climbed up the stairs. He knew she wanted him to scream and curse at her, but he said nothing. There was only the sound of her breathing and the clacking of her high-heeled shoes filling the air.

"Mistress," Conrad called from the top of the stairs.

Alaric's attention focused on him as he saw him offering his hand to help her.

"Are you sure he won't be able to escape?" she whispered.

Alaric smirked at her fear.

Marie voiced her concerns once again, "Are you sure the caretaker is loyal to us?"

"No one will find him here, and we are free to go wherever you want."

Marie nodded, accepting his arms around her waist. She turned around to close the heavy door. Alaric saw Conrad kissing her cheek as he rubbed her belly.

He inhaled harshly, stepping back. He focused his hearing on them, expecting to hear something useful to understand where he was being detained.

Marie said, "I can't believe that I'm free."

"We can go wherever you want," Conrad said.

"I want to go back home… I miss it there."

"Wherever you want, my love."

The door closed and the key turned to lock it. Alaric was left alone in the darkness.

**THE END**

*Please leave a review if you enjoyed this book. Reviews are essential for Indie Authors.*

*Sign up for my Newsletter to get a notification the day a new book comes out and find more about my other books and giveaways.*

# COMING SOON — SHATTERED

## SHATTERED
### BOOK 4 OF THE IMMORTAL LOVE SERIES

## Extended Summary

For centuries, Beth and her sister Marie dreamed of finding their soul-mates. But all their dreams are shattered when the person who should love and take care of Marie ends up to be the cruelest of the monsters.

After being held captive for several years by the lunatic vampire who had fun abusing and torturing her, Beth is rescued from the endless nightmare she had been living. Only to find out that her soul-mate is the youngest brother of the vampire she hates the most in the whole world–her tormentor and Marie's mate.

Eric dreams of finding his soul-mate for almost two hundred years. When his family tries to apprehend his older brother Alaric, his wish comes true but with a price. His mate is terrified of him and males in general because of what his brother did to her. Eric needs to win her trust and make her believe that he's nothing like Alaric and he would never hurt her.

Beth believes that her soul is damaged beyond repair. *Can Eric fix her or are they doomed to be alone forever?*

## You can sign up to know when this book is available/in pre-order.
## <u>TAP HERE</u>
## And don't forget to read, next, the first chapter of a new paranormal romance series that is coming in 2017.

# PREVIEW—HIS BELOVED

## ONE—THE SELECTION

The last thing Jade wanted was to follow her best friend, Jenna, to that fancy nightclub. There, people begged and did anything to get picked by a vampire so they could be turned or become their personal pet for a week. She sure didn't want to be one—a vampire, or a pet. Her favorite color was pink for God's sake! She also didn't like reality shows, and 'Who wants to be a vampire?' was the most pathetic of them all.

"I can't believe I let you talk me into this," Jade complained, leveling her voice so Jenna heard her, despite the loud boom of music and chatter.

"That's what friends are for, to talk you into doing something you would never do," Jenna argued.

Jade rolled her eyes, drinking her non-alcoholic beverage through a straw.

"Just relax! You are here to keep me company. Nothing bad will happen. These are friendly vampires."

"Right!" Jade replied. "I can't believe there are so many people paying for this!"

"It's a really famous reality show. You have no idea how many people want to be a vampire."

"I have no idea why." Jade shrugged. "Vampires are dead, they can't come out into the sun and they have to drink blood to keep living," she said, folding a finger for every reason she named. "They are evil creatures, who think they are better than the rest of us. They use these people for sex and blood, only to discard them and choose someone new the next week."

Jenna kept smiling, and Jade knew she had voiced the same argument countless times, portraying her dislike for the undead.

"What else did I forget? Who in their right mind wants to be a vampire?"

Jenna puckered her lips before replying to the rhetorical question. "Jade, a lot of people would beg to differ with you.

"Why? Because they are immortal? Maybe they can live for a long time, but they can be killed."

"Keep it down," Jenna mumbled, looking around to see if anyone overheard them. "The last thing we want is for you to be kicked out of the club!"

Jade lowered her voice. "In my opinion, having to drink blood is pretty much a deal-breaker. Besides, they don't actually choose anyone to spend their eternity with." She air quoted eternity. "How many humans have been turned or chosen to be their beloveds since the show began?"

Jenna shrugged. "I just want to meet Seth."

Jade kept rambling. "I just think it's scary how many humans treat them as if they are gods and are willing to be used just to appear on TV."

Some girls next to the stage started screaming over the music, silencing Jenna's retort. She frantically looked around as she rested her hands on her chest. "They have arrived," she mumbled, breathless.

"I'll be fine. Just go look for the vampire of your dreams, even if I think you deserve a lot better than a bloodsucking, arrogant, and smelly corpse."

With a giggle, Jade put her hands on Jade's shoulders. "I'll come find you in a bit. I just need to see Seth and the others. Who knows, they might pick me!"

With a shrug, Jade scanned the club for a safe place to stay out of sight while her friend went to flirt and try to find a sexy vampire willing to adopt her. She chose the darkest corner, away from the crowd of dancing bodies and humans desperate for some attention. The scariest of the supporters had a picture of one of the vampires—Seth—on their chest like some kind of treasure. Of course, he was gorgeous and famous. Of course, they would only pick the dazzling undead to be the main attraction in the show. There was no point in choosing ugly and old-looking vampires. It wouldn't sell, and people wouldn't line up to be chosen.

The show had seven vampires, each one known for being a singer, an actor, or just a famous socialite. Seth was the most famous of them all because he had once been the lead singer in some boy band. She wasn't sure anymore which because it's been awhile since he was famous for his vocals. Now he was well-known for doing low-budget movies and for being a hot vamp. He was going by the name of 'Seth' for the last few decades, with his perfect curly hair and deep blue eyes.

Since Jade wasn't remotely interested in being turned or a vampire pet, she didn't need to worry about looking pretty when she got dressed to come here. She was just fine in her pink tank top and her blue pair of skinny jeans. Actually, the last thing she wanted was to catch the attention of one of these men. After the selection, she could go back home and resume her quiet existence.

Jade massaged her temples with all the screaming and colorful lights. Meanwhile, Jenna was nowhere to be found. She was probably making out with one of those creepy cold bloodsuckers. The thought made her cringe. The whole idea of exchanging saliva with a being that drank blood was all but appealing.

Someone cleared their throat behind her. "Excuse me."

It was a man's voice, and it scared the crap out of her.

Startled, she jumped and held her hands to her chest while her heart raced and almost beat out of her chest. She thought she was all alone and safe from danger. So, how could someone be there? There was a wall behind her!

"You are in my way," the man said as Jade turned around and saw an open door behind the guy.

She could have sworn the door wasn't there before. Her vision narrowed on the guy in front of her. Her face was just in front of his chest—a rather sculptured and interesting chest. He was wearing a black cotton sweater that molded his ripped torso perfectly. He even smelled nice, probably because of some ridiculously expensive men's cologne.

"So"—the guy sighed with impatience—"are you moving?"

Jade blushed for acting so silly and standing like a statue in front of him. Finding her voice, she apologized, only to lose her voice again when she perceived his serious face—his heavenly, gorgeous, and breathless face with a stunning pair of piercing blue eyes. Her mouth went dry and her palms perspired as she moved to one side to let him pass. Then she noticed his messily styled, shiny, raven hair, making him appear even sexier. He might be gorgeous but he was also rude and grumpy.

He didn't even give her a second glance or thank her.

"Annoying human groupies," he growled between his teeth and moved forward, leaving behind a trail of woody, herbal, and fruity notes caressing the air she was breathing.

Because of his words, she instantly understood what he was. Her fascination quickly dissipated. There it was: the arrogance and the rudeness. He could be attractive, but he was an asshole. He was probably late to find some blonde chick so he could have his late night snack. She chased away her urge to gag.

Jade didn't have time to make any more assumptions because a cute little teen girl with golden locks came out from the same hidden entrance. She was pretty, but had a really odd taste in clothes. The girl looked like a cartoon character straight out of a manga in her short, black Victorian doll dress and a magician's hat. Lace gloved covered her hands, completing the outfit. However, unlike Mr. Rude from earlier, she shot Jade a smile and winked with a happy giggle.

The door closed with a swift movement and all that

was left was the wall. It had to be a secret passage of some sort.

Jade sighed deeply. She had no peace there. She couldn't even be safe in some faraway corner without a vampire showing up and creeping her out! She leaned back and took out her phone, distracting herself. Despite her efforts to keep a low profile, some guys came up to her, asking her to dance or offering her drinks. She refused everything, more interested in knowing when Jenna would show up so they could leave. Sometimes, she browsed the crowd, looking for her best friend. However, she knew that she had to wait for the selection to end for Jenna to want to leave this place.

"Hi," a male voice said, trying to get her attention.

Without taking her eyes off the game she was playing on her phone, she replied loud enough for him to hear, "I'm not interested."

"I just need you to move so I can go inside," he said, making Jade raise her eyes from her screen and look at him.

It was the same rude vamp again. For a few seconds, it was hard for her to move her gaze away from his. She had seen him around, not very far from the place he had crawled out of. He had been talking with people in the VIP area. He didn't seem to want to be there. It was something that they had in common, but it didn't make him less of a jerk. The proof was in the way he was now staring at her as if she was an inconvenience.

"I'm not even near the door," she muttered, looking sideways to a couple that was obstructing his secret door.

"The panel to open the door is behind you," he explained, moving forward to reach for it. Jade retreated, panicked by the closeness.

"Personal space," she complained and tried to evade the touch of his arm. The last thing she wanted was to be touched by a bloodsucking monster.

"Why do you smell so good?" he whispered close to her ear, sending unwelcome shivers down her spine. Listening to such words from a vampire wasn't on her bucket list. She could feel his presence and she was sure that there was no panel behind her because she didn't hear the door opening.

"What's your name?" he asked, backing away.

"Again," she said, picking up the courage to face him. "I'm not interested. Now could you move so I can leave?"

He narrowed his eyes and clenched his teeth. Jade gulped, unsure if he was going to do something to hurt her. Vampires were unpredictable, and she had just wounded his enormous ego—she was sure of it.

Seconds later, he touched his ear and smirked like a sexy demon. "We'll talk later, Jade. Don't go too far."

Her blood fled from her face once her name left his mouth. He touched his phone and the door opened. The people around them moved so he could enter, and Jade ran from where she was to look for Jenna.

Half an hour later, she was still feeling uncomfortable with the fact that a vampire knew her name and had shown an interest in her. Meanwhile, Jenna was nowhere to be found and the amount of people inside that place was making Jade feel claustrophobic.

Suddenly, a loud squealing sound of a mic made everybody shut up for a while. It was time for the show. Young women and men would be picked and taken by their new vampire masters. The host—a vampire man— would go to the stage area and read out names or point at the crowd. Some screaming and hysterical members of the audience would be thrilled to become a vampire's snack and have a shot at convincing one to turn them. Nothing new about that scenario.

It was a clever idea. She had to give them credit, to the vampires, not the humans. They didn't need to hunt for food. Food walked straight through their front door and begged them to be eaten. They even profited with the money people paid to get in and the revenue from the show that was broadcasted live to the entire country every Sunday night. Only in sponsorship, the reality show earned a crazy amount of money, making it one of the most popular and seen programs in the world! *Crazy, right?*

Jade always got sick when thinking about it. At least, deaths by vampire attacks were diminishing and the vampire population was under control because it was rare for them to actually turn someone. They just used the show as bait to make people donate their bodies and their blood willingly with a smile on their lips for a vague promise of immortality.

As expected, after a lot of talking and the drama with vampires saying goodbye to the older pets, the show's host began to pair new humans, by calling their names, with the vampires who were waiting on stage. It was normally the same vampires every week, and every week they left with someone new.

When the chosen girls were brought to the stage, they hugged each other like best friends and screamed and jumped like they had just won the Miss Universe Pageant.

This night was a complete waste of time. Jade had better things to do. She didn't even watch this show on TV! *How did she get convinced by Jenna to come here?* Right, Jenna had promised to take Stevie to school for a whole month. At least, it was almost over and she could go home.

"And now, the sponsor of this party will pick one of you to spend an entire week with him and maybe turn you into his beloved. You heard me right! His beloved! Our famous bachelor is looking for a companion for an eternity! You can be the lucky one," the show's host happily informed, pointing a finger at the crowd and making girls release shrieks of excitement.

*More propaganda and more empty promises of some new vampire added to the team.* Jade stared at the stage, impatient, almost becoming deaf with the screams and shouts the girls were producing so the eligible vampire bachelor would pick them.

"Did you hear that?" Jenna mysteriously appeared next to Jade, gripping her arm tightly while jumping in her tiny sexy red dress and making her hair bounce up and down together with her boobs. Jenna was pretty and blonde, maybe she would get picked and would stop getting Jade into trouble and inside parties like this one. But then Jade would miss her best friend!

"We can still be picked!" Jenna said enthusiastically, and Jade stared at her with a grumpy face.

"I'm not blonde and I don't want to be picked. I'm here against my will."

"Oh, stop being such an old lady and have fun!"

Jade was going to answer her, but something caught her attention from the corner of her eye. On the stage, a tall, black-haired vampire stepped forward and with his blue, piercing eyes and stared coldly at the crowd. Jade's heart almost stopped in her chest when she recognized him as the one who tried to seduce her and scared her senseless by knowing her name. If he was the sponsor of the party that meant the nightclub was his and that was why he had a secret doorway in the wall.

Something inside her stomach clenched at the idea that he was going to be part of that freak show.

Jade had no idea she was staring fixedly at him until Jenna talked into her ear. "He's hot, isn't he? This is so exciting!"

Jenna shook Jade, making her dizzy.

"I really want to go back home," she mumbled, noticing how his arrival had made everybody go quiet, waiting for him to speak.

Meanwhile, on the stage, the vampire looked intimidating. He was really serious, manipulating the suspense of who was going to be his victim. His eyes scanned the crowd, once, twice. Many girls were holding their breaths while Jade tried to free her arm from Jenna's hold. She was hurting her.

"This is stupid! I'm leaving," Jade said between her teeth and pushed Jenna away.

She was about to leave when she heard a creepy and authoritative voice say, "You!"

The vampire had picked his new prey. She couldn't care less about who the poor bastard was. She just sighed, bit her nail, and stared at Jenna.

"Can we go now?"

However, Jenna was really quiet and serious as if in shock. When Jade looked at the silent crowd, a bunch of people was staring at them both. It was not just her impression, they were really staring at them.

"Me?" Jenna asked, suddenly shy. She was clearly looking at and talking to the vampire.

Her breath caught in her throat as she became static. She was losing her best friend to a vampire! *What horrors would she experience in his company?*

"No!" The vampire's answer sounded like a lightning bolt hitting the ground. "You," he said with a renewed strong and powerful voice, which made Jenna stare at Jade, and Jade stare at the stage, noticing his finger pointing in her direction.

*Was he choosing her? No way!* He had to be kidding. *Was that a sick joke?*

"Come again?" Jade asked, swallowing hard and feeling the ground disappearing under her feet.

"And here you have it folks, the girl has been chosen," the host said, sharing the good news with the rest.

Everybody cheered around them. The music started playing again, and Jade's ability to breathe was suspended while she was staring at the vampire in horror.

"Go get her!" the vampire ordered, and the spotlights of the cameras followed the two big, strong men in expensive, gray, Italian suits. They were probably his bodyguards.

"But I'm not even a cute blonde!" Jade complained, not believing in what was happening to her. She didn't have any time to think about it because the duo held her up by the arms and took her to their master.

# MORE ABOUT THE AUTHOR

Anna Santos is a Bestselling Author in Paranormal Romance.

Anna always keeps her readers on their toes with her adrenaline-fueled adventures, suspense-filled cliffhangers, and romantic scenes.

When she isn't writing, Anna is considering plot twists for her next novel or delving into the world of her favorite authors. She loves superheroes, and she's a geek at heart. She grew up watching *Star Wars* and plotting a way to become a Ninja. She has a fascination for Chinese Kung Fu movies and cherry blossom flowers.

She also enjoys writing poetry, watching a good movie, and spending time with her husband and family.

Meanwhile, there's more to come, and if you'd like to know about it, you can join her at:

http://www.annasantosauthor.com
https://www.facebook.com/AnnaSantosAuthor
https://twitter.com/AnneSaint90
https://instagram.com/annasantosauthor
https://www.wattpad.com/user/AnnaSantos5

**You can sign-up for Anna's newsletter here:**

https://app.mailerlite.com/webforms/landing/w4r0o1